Author's Note

The stories contained in this volume represent numerous time periods and locales. Some of the ideas in them are no longer considered appropriate, but were true to their time and place.

Pocketful of Stories: The Omnibus Edition

Sharon E. Cathcart

Published by Sharon E. Cathcart, 2022.

Last Stop: Storyville

There were few things Jimmy Arceneaux liked more than having his girlfriend, Cindy, touch his hair.

He said as much while Cindy braided his shiny black locks as they sat under the Mardi Gras oak at Tulane University, where Jimmy was in his first year of pre-med. Jimmy's hair hung just past his shoulder blades; he'd been growing it since his first day of high school, when he informed his hairdresser mother that he didn't want a haircut for school that year. The agreement was that as long as he took care of it, that was fine. The end result was that Jimmy's hair was the envy of just about every woman he met.

Jimmy stayed with his great aunt, Julie, who lived in a camelback shotgun house around the corner from campus. She was out of town, and the only company Jimmy had just then were her two cats, Teddy and Timmy. "They're sweet cats, but not good at keeping their end of the conversation."

Cindy promptly invited him to dinner that evening.

"I'll catch the streetcar and come on over," he said.

The Landrys lived just off of Rampart on St. Philips Street. It was an easy trip on the streetcar; he would have to walk a couple of blocks past the usual dive bars and tourist voodoo shops, but that was the French Quarter these days in a nutshell.

Jimmy tapped on the Landrys' door, hoping he didn't look too sloppy. Jeans and sneakers were okay for goofing off on a summer's day, but maybe not for dinner. He also hoped that the summer heat hadn't left him smelling bad.

Cindy, wearing a flowered blouse and jeans, answered the door and gave her boyfriend a kiss. "I can't wait for you to meet the family !".

"I probably should have dressed up more." Jimmy looked down at the floor.

"Don't be silly. They'll love you."

Cindy kept up a running chatter as she showed Jimmy around the house. Her father, Jack, had just put the salad bowl on the table, but stopped and shook the newcomer's hand. Jack looked Jimmy up and down over the rims of his glasses.

"We've heard a lot about you, son. It's nice to meet you at last."

"My pleasure, sir. Truly."

Helene Landry followed with a big dish of jambalaya. Like Cindy, she was blonde and petite.

"My daughter didn't tell me her new fellow was so handsome. Please take this, would you? I'll get the lemonade." She handed the serving dish to Jimmy, and he placed it in the center of the table.

Dinner conversation was easy and light, which was a relief. After the meal, Jimmy insisted on helping with the dishes.

"All I have to do is load the dishwasher."

"A good guest helps clean up."

Helene and Jack exchanged a look; it was clear that they were impressed.

After visiting for another hour or so, Jimmy took his leave.

"It's time I head back home. Thank you for dinner, and the great conversation. It was a real pleasure to meet all of you." Jimmy hugged Helene and shook Jack's hand, kissing Cindy on the cheek before showing himself out.

The clear skies had turned rainy while he was inside, as happened more days than not in New Orleans. Rather than walking over to Canal Street, Jimmy decided to take the Rampart Street line and connect to the St. Charles line from there to go home. He walked up to Armstrong Park and got on the red streetcar, number 13 emblazoned on the front disc. Settling into the mahogany seat, he realized how tired he was. It would be good to get home and get some sleep.

♨ ॐ

He jerked awake when the driver announced "Last stop, Basin Street." He let himself out of the green streetcar and shook his head. Everything looked different; none of the Canal Street hotels were lit up. He wiped his eyes and looked around, trying to get his bearings.

A voice came from the nearby alleyway. "Hey, Injun boy. You might want to get back of town where you belong."

The next thing Jimmy heard was the snick of an opening switchblade knife. Out of the alley between a couple of one-room shanties came two men who had clearly had too much to drink. Their pants were held up by suspenders, and they seemed to be wearing long johns. What on earth was going on?

"I'm not Indian, I'm Cajun," Jimmy replied.

"Even worse," said the man who held the knife. "You need to get your coonass self back to the swamp."

A third man grabbed Jimmy from behind and pushed him down on his knees in the dust.

Dust? It was raining just minutes ago. Why was the ground dry?

"I'll call the police." Jimmy looked up at them, his eyes hard.

"Police? Here? That's a laugh. Tom Anderson's got them all in his pocket, and he don't like Injuns or Cajuns or coloreds hangin' around — unless the colored fella is playin' the pian-y in one of the parlor houses. And you don't look like no whorehouse pian-y player, neither. You look like an Injun to me, with that braid goin' down your back."

Whorehouses?

"I think this Injun needs to be scalped," the second man said, taking a swig from a flask. He grabbed Jimmy's braid and held it up. "What do you fellers think?"

Please, God, don't let them kill me. He jutted his chin out, determined not to let them see his fear.

"Well, I reckon we can help him look decent by givin' him a haircut," the man with the knife sneered. "You hold him still."

Two of the men held Jimmy while he tried struggling to his feet. They pushed him back to the ground. In seconds, Jimmy's braid was thrown down in front of him, raising a puff of dust.

"Now get back to where you belong," the third man said, shoving him toward Rampart Street. He picked up the braid and said "Reckon this'll make a nice fob for my Sunday watch chain," and they all walked away, laughing and patting each other on the back.

"Are they gone?" A young woman stood in the door of one of the cabins. She wore nothing but a one-piece undergarment and a pair of flat shoes. She looked a little like Cindy, blonde and petite, but careworn.

"Yes, they are."

"You're lucky that they didn't do more to you than just haircuttin'. The men who come around here aren't the nice ones who go to Josie Arlington's to hear Professor Jellyroll Morton play piano, if you catch my meaning."

"I'm Jimmy Arceneaux," he said, offering a hand to her. "And you are?"

"Lucy. Just ... Lucy." She took his hand. "Come on in here. It ain't much, but you can at least brush your clothes off and I can maybe fix what they done to your hair. I used to cut my daddy's and my brothers' hair when I still lived at home."

Jimmy entered Lucy's cabin, just one room with a bed, a pitcher and ewer in a stand, a table and a chair. An oil lamp on the table was the only light. A faded calico dress hung on a wall peg. His jaw dropped. Where were the electrical outlets? Where was the bathroom?

"What's the matter, Jimmy Arceneaux? Ain't you never seen a whore's crib before?"

"What year is it?" Jimmy asked.

"Are you sure they didn't hit you in the head or somethin'? It's 1916."

Lucy pulled a carpet bag from under the bed and rummaged around until she pulled out a comb and a pair of scissors.

"Have a seat," she said. "You'll want to take off that fancy shirt or there'll be hair all over it. We'll worry about the knees of your pants later."

Jimmy took off his shirt and Lucy hung it on the peg next to her dress.

"You're a beautiful woman," he said. "Why ..."

"Never you mind why. Let's just say that I need to eat, same as anyone else."

She combed and cut, swaths of dark hair landing on the floor and on Jimmy's shoulders. He was pretty sure his hair was going to be shorter than he wanted. Hell, with the braid gone he had to do something. Still, it felt just as good when Lucy touched his hair as when Cindy did it ... and it would grow.

"You're a nice-lookin' fella yourself," Lucy said as she trimmed the hair around his ears. "Don't know why you had your hair like that."

She looked at him again, hard. "How old are you?"

"I'm 19, ma'am. I go to Tulane University, studying to be a doctor."

"Boy, you surely are on the wrong side of the tracks, ain't you? What the hell brought you to Storyville?"

Jimmy had no answer.

"Well, anyway, you'll pass in decent society again."

Lucy pulled a little mirror out of her bag and handed it to Jimmy. He hadn't realized until that moment, with his hair cut short, how much he looked like his favorite uncle.

"Thank you, Lucy." Jimmy brushed ineffectively at the knees of his pants, but the dust and dirt were ground in. "I need to be going."

"No, sir, you do not. Take off them pants and I'll brush them later. Then, as long as you've got your pants off, you might as well come on over and get your two bits' worth from me ..."

"I've never ..."

"Been with a whore?"

"No, ma'am. Been with a woman." Jimmy could feel the heat creeping up his neck and ears.

"Lay off that ma'am nonsense. I'm just Lucy, hear? And take off them pants. I won't even charge you the quarter; I ain't never had the chance to teach a pretty boy like you. You wash yourself in that basin; the blue stuff in there's disinfectant. Then you come on over to this bed."

Jimmy fell asleep after surrendering his virginity. He was embarrassed when he woke up and found Lucy sketching him. Still, he craned his neck.

"You can see when I'm done." She took a few more minutes to complete her drawing and then turned the pad around to show him.

"Lord-a-mercy." She'd captured his cheekbones and slender nose perfectly, his hair mussed as he slept with an arm under the pillow. "You sure made me look like an uncle of mine."

"He must be one helluva handsome man," she laughed.

"The ladies always seem to think so," Jimmy smiled. Then he turned serious. "Look, Lucy, you've got talent. That's a beautiful drawing. Haven't you ever thought about making a living from your art?"

"In case you ain't noticed, jobs are few and far between right now," she replied. "That's exactly why I came here in the first place. Thought I could get me a job drawing for the Times or something. That didn't exactly turn out. I ran out of money, and I had to leave the boarding house. I wasn't pretty enough for one of the fancy houses, but I can rent me one of these cribs from Tom Anderson for twenty-five cents a day. All that takes is one trick, so anything else is gravy."

"How much is rent at the boarding house," Jimmy asked

"Five dollars a week."

Jimmy got out of bed and pulled on his pants. He took his wallet out of the back pocket and pulled out some bills, which he put on the table without even considering whether they'd be any good in 1916. Then, he put on his shirt and shoes.

"Here's eight weeks' rent, Lucy. Get out of this life."

He walked out the door with just one backward glance. Lucy stood in the door, a sad expression on her pretty face as Jimmy caught the green Canal Street streetcar. He took it as far as Common, where he switched to the St. Charles line and went home.

❧

Jimmy awoke in the attic bedroom of Tante Julie's house, shaking his head as though it would loosen memories of that peculiar dream. He thought Cindy would get a laugh out of it.

He padded down the hall to the bathroom, splashed some water onto his face, and looked up into the mirror. His hair was cut short, a trifle uneven ... as though someone with no training had taken the shears to his black locks.

His shocked cursing awoke the cats.

Yellowjack and the River Man

Fever Dreams

New Orleans
    1844

Alcide Devereaux had no idea what day it was. He lay under the mosquito barre, tossing and turning. Sometimes he slept, but his dreams were passing strange.

The day he vomited brown, Alcide sent the entire household out to the plantation and tacked the yellow card on the door of their Rampart Street home himself. He left the plank out over the gutter so the undertakers could get his body out.

Yellow Jack. Bronze John.

No matter what they called it, Alcide had it. He was sure he'd join his beloved Evangeline soon. She'd died giving birth to Victoire, their four-year-old spitfire of a daughter. At least she would be well cared for by her grandmother, Jeannette Devereaux and, eventually, her older siblings.

To prevent infection in the house to which his family would return, Alcide removed himself to the garçonniere where he'd lived as a young man. The narrow, iron-framed bed creaked as he squirmed, sweat pouring from his fever-stricken body. The chamber pot was barely used except to catch his vomit.

He'd given up wearing anything but a linen night shirt, and lay atop the moss-filled mattress with only a sheet beneath him. Bedclothes were tossed on the floor at the foot; the weight of even the lightest quilt was unbearable.

Alcide was, in a word, waiting to die.

The universe, however, had different plans.

❧ ☙

Marie Laveau had passed so many houses with yellow tags on the door that she no longer paid them any mind. The writing was irrelevant; she couldn't read. Besides, the color of the card told her everything she needed to know; someone inside was dying of yellow fever.

Still, seeing a card on the Devereaux house drew her up short. There wasn't a person of color in the Quarter who didn't know about Michie Alcide's work on their behalf. In fact, there were no small number who had gone North with his help, some with forged free papers or new identities that allowed them to pass.

Marie was one of the few who knew what they called the steamboat pilot turned lawyer on the Underground Railroad: River Man.

Marie knew the latch would be open; eventually, undertakers had to get the bodies out of fever houses. So, she wasn't shy about opening the door. She'd gone to the house many times to fix Madame Evangeline's hair before the poor woman passed, and knew her way around.

Both the men's and the women's side of the house were empty, so she went out to the courtyard. The stove in the cookhouse was still warm, although the fire was almost out. There was a stack of good wood to stoke it, should the need arise, but there was no one in the yard.

A low moan issued from another little outbuilding; Marie didn't hesitate to walk in.

Might have known there'd be a garçonniere. Works good as a plague house, too.

She pushed the mosquito barre aside, and didn't even bat an eye. Neither Alcide's near-nudity nor the stench of the sickroom were a deterrent.

"Michie Alcide, it's me, Mam'zelle Marie. I imagine you don't know me right now, but you will."

She went back out to the cookhouse and put some tinder and kindling in the stove to get the fire going again. Water pulled from the covered well proved fresh and clear, with no bugs in it. Marie put a kettle on to boil and added more wood to the fire. Rifling through the cook's cabinet gave her grains to make a thin gruel.

Back into the house to search the men's armoires for a clean nightshirt and the shaving things.

Eventually he'll want them and best he not have to walk far.

She also pulled a few washcloths from a stack on the stand and took the pitcher, bowl and soap with her when she went back to the garçonniere.

Pulling scissors from her basket, she cut the nightshirt away from Alcide's body. She found sheets in a cabinet and changed the one beneath him as deftly as a hospital nurse. Sheet, shirt, and chamber pot contents were disposed of in the outhouse and covered with quicklime from a nearby bucket.

Marie poured some of the warm water from the kettle into the china pitcher on her second trip to the cook house, and mixed some more of it with the grain in a smaller pan. By the time she was done washing down Alcide's pale, muscular form, it was ready to eat. She carried a gourd and wooden spoon with her into the room.

"Michie Devereaux, I'm going to help you sit up." She positioned pillows against the bedframe.

Alcide stared blankly at the copper-skinned woman with her seven-pointed tignon.

"Yellow Jack," he gasped. "Go!"

"No, Michie Alcide. I'm here to help you."

She was surprisingly strong, and Alcide greatly weakened. Marie slid him up the clean sheet to a seated position and fed him the gruel tiny spoonfuls at a time.

"You tell me if you need to make sick and we'll stop."

Somehow, everything stayed down.

"Maybe we should call a doctor." Alcide could barely speak.

"And let them fill you with that calomel poison? Michie Devereaux, that mess kills more people than it cures. Anyway, I think you may be through the worst of it. We'll see. But your skin and eyes aren't yellow, so that's something. Now put on this clean nightshirt and lie down. You need to keep this quilt over you, too."

Alcide obeyed without hesitation. Once he was under the covers, Marie promised him the she or one of her children would be by to check on him every few hours.

"Why?" he asked.

"Because, River Man, you been good to my people. I am not afraid of Michie Bronze John, but we are all afraid of what might happen if we lose Michie Alcide Devereaux."

Marie was true to her word, and before long Alcide felt better, if still weak. Eventually he wrote to his family and asked them to come home.

On that same day, he asked Marie to cut his hair and help him shave. Though she usually only did ladies' hair, she agreed.

"Do you know anything about dreams, Mam'zelle Marie," he asked as she snipped at his black locks.

"Some."

"I kept dreaming that Evangeline was next to me in bed, except her hair was brown and short like a man's. She was with child and I could see my hand touching her belly ... only it didn't look like my hand. It had on a heavy gold ring covering a tattoo. I knew we were in New Orleans, but it wasn't this house. And I knew she was having a hard time with her pregnancy but that she'd make it. I dreamt it over and over; it was like I was looking through someone else's eyes."

"How did you feel when you dreamed that?"

Alcide considered for a while before answering. "I felt satisfied."

"Then I think it was a good dream, Michie Alcide. A dream about future days."

Marie cleaned up the hair-cutting things and put them away. Alcide pressed several bank notes into the voodoo queen's hand and wouldn't take "no" for an answer.

The River Man

Vacherie

April 1863

Alcide Devereaux rubbed the grizzled stubble on his chin. He mentally apologized to Evangeline; she'd always preferred him clean-shaven. Even though she'd been gone for more than twenty years, Alcide still kept his face smooth, regardless of the fashion.

There was only one exception. At 57 years of age, Alcide still worked as a conductor; when there was a delivery to make, he avoided his razor for several days in advance. His craggy, unshaven face, greying dark hair, and a ragged old hat with a red turkey feather proclaimed him an aging riverboat tough. The strip of black-dyed fabric tied around his shirt-sleeve declared him a man in mourning.

Alcide had worn a band of black around his hard-muscled arm since the day Evangeline died giving birth to Victoire, their youngest of five living children.

At 23 years of age, Victoire managed the Devereaux sugar plantation. With men dead left and right, including her eldest brother Henri, Victoire's prospects for marriage were few.

Henri's death still rankled. None of the Blacks on the Devereaux place were slaves anymore; Alcide had freed them himself. Henri and his valet, a free-born man named Guillaume, were shot out on the River Road by a gang of poor whites who wanted their mounts.

When Alcide's famous black horses were recognized by the sheriff, he was more than happy to press charges. Then, he stood quietly and watched his son's murderers hanged for the lesser crime of horse theft and wondered at the strangeness of the world. He could never have foreseen people going to war over the right to own other human beings.

It was for that reason that he took up his role with the Underground Railroad again. He'd given it up when Henri was born, content to stay home with his family.

Now his first-born and his wife were both gone. The Railroad was all that gave him purpose. Alcide spent several days restoring his old, false-bottomed wagon. He bought a raw-boned sorrel jack mule he called Bill, and filled the wagon bed with all kinds of junk. With the ragged clothes he wore, and his scruffy appearance, even long-time friends would be hard-pressed to recognize the elegant Creole widower beneath the raggedy tinker.

With eligible men few and far between, there were whispers about Alcide's continued mourning. Most men put it off after the so-called decent interval of three years. Surely one of the local widows, young or old, might have caught his eye. And yet this was not the case at all. He'd yet to meet another woman who expressed the abolitionist tendencies that time spent in Paris had bred in his Evangeline.

In fact, tonight he and his wagon were waiting under the live oaks for a family of slaves from a neighboring plantation. The owner was herself a widow, and her treatment of the slaves on her land was horrific.

Bill stamped the ground impatiently. Every buckle on his harness was wrapped in cloth so the metal would make no sound. Come daylight, the fabric would be removed to reveal worn metal and cracking leather. The mule and junk wagon carried precious cargo, but couldn't look better than the wagoneer. Anything to avoid suspicion.

A rustle in the grass, then a quiet male voice.

"You the River Man, suh?"

None of the conductors used their real names. The work they did was a crime punishable by death because of the Fugitive Slave Act, and they could not risk being known.

"That's me. You'd be from the Delatoire place?"

"Yassuh."

Alcide stepped down from the driver's seat to help the man, woman, and little girl into the hidden compartment in the wagon bed. He slipped forged freedom papers into the man's hand

"Next stop, I'll hand you over to the Man from Paris, in New Orleans." Alcide closed the panel. Alcide stepped back on board the wagon and clucked his tongue at Bill, who stepped off with significantly less style than Alcide's favorite mare had done in the days when he courted Evangeline.

"I hope you're still proud of me, my love," he whispered as the mule picked up a trot under the moonlight.

As they moved out, he made a silent prayer for the safety of his cargo.

An Unexpected Visit

December 25, 1867

New Orleans

"No, Martine, I insist. Go home and spend the day with your family."

"Michie Alcide. It isn't right, you sittin' up in here alone on Christmas."

Alcide stood up from his chair and helped Martine on with her coat.

"I won't be alone. I'm dining at Maspero's, and going to Mass at Saint Anthony's. Go home, and have a merry Christmas."

"There's ham warming on the stove and a loaf of bread I just made if you want to fix yourself a sandwich. I don't like leaving you by yourself, all the same."

"You're a kind woman." Alcide hugged his dark-skinned servant. "Your husband is a lucky man. Now, go."

Alcide closed the door behind her and watched her through the window as she walked down Rampart Street toward her home.

Christmas did seem odd with the house empty. The children were all far away, living their own lives. Evangeline ... God, was it possible she'd been gone more than twenty-five years? No woman had ever captured his attention, let alone his heart, the way she did.

Alcide was about to step away from the window when he noticed a slender young man standing at the door, looking back and forth between a slip of paper and the house number.

Alcide opened the door, startling the fellow.

"May I help you? You look like you might be lost."

"Monsieur Devereaux?"

"I am he."

"I know, sir. You don't look so very different from the last time I saw you," he replied. "My name is Henri de la Vega. My mother's name was Natalie."

My brother's boy. I haven't seen him since he was a child.

"Please, come in," Alcide said. "I was about to fix myself a sandwich. Maybe you can join me?"

"I'd be honored. Chicago was a long ways back, and the food on the train was dear."

Henri scraped his boots before entering. Inside, he took off his hat and looked around.

"My maid has the day off for Christmas. Please, come with me out to the kitchen. Leave your hat on the table."

Henri followed his uncle through the house and into the courtyard. Alcide was still tall and slim; his black hair had gone entirely silver, but his eyes were sharp and clear. A black band around Alcide's shirtsleeve marked him as a man in mourning.

"I am sorry for your loss, sir. My mother passed away a few years ago and I've only just come out of mourning myself."

Alcide touched the black silk around his arm.

"I've worn this since the day I lost Evangeline." His eyes were glassy with unshed tears. "I'm sorry to hear about Natalie."

"She had a good life. She married a gentleman she met at the grocery, of all places." He paused. "A white man. Your papers gave us a good life."

"I am glad to know that."

Alcide cut four slices of bread, buttered them, and added thick slabs of ham. He put the sandwiches on plates and brought them to a small table near the stove.

"We can eat out here if that's all right. The stove is warm, and thank God there's no rain. I want to hear about how you've done since I put you and your mother on that train all those years ago."

Henri told him about growing up in Chicago, where no one knew of his mother's "colored" blood. The grocer Natalie married, Guillermo Natale, was Italian; he saw no problem marrying a pretty Spanish widow whose quiet young son could help around the store.

And then he and Natalie died, victims of an influenza epidemic.

"He didn't leave the store to you?"

"No. He was married before and widowed; the store went to his eldest son. So, I worked there while I saved money to return to New Orleans."

Alcide took a bite of his sandwich.

"What will you do?"

"I don't know, to be honest. I know how to read, write, and cipher. I am not afraid of hard work. I can run a store ... I can clerk for you."

"I don't have many clients these days."

"I see." Henri picked up his sandwich and took a bite, chewing thoughtfully before he spoke again.

"Perhaps you know a grocery man I could work for. I have a room over on Common Street, and my money will last while I look for work if I'm careful ... but I will need to find something."

"I will give some thought to the matter," Alcide promised.

The two finished their sandwiches and went back into the main house. Henri collected his hat and prepared to say his farewells.

"Thank you for seeing me today, Monsieur Devereaux."

"Please join me for dinner at Maspero's at seven o'clock," the older man replied. "We can go to Mass together afterward."

"That's a bit dear for my purse." Henri sounded rueful.

"You are my guest for the evening, Henri. Consider it a Christmas gift."

"In that case, it would be an honor. I will see you then, sir."

After Henri left, Alcide went to his office and pulled some documents from the filing cabinet. He sat a pair of pince-nez on his nose and read the materials carefully. Then he started to write, periodically consulting a law book before putting pen back to paper.

By the time Alcide was satisfied with the documents, it was approaching six o'clock. He stretched, rubbed his eyes, and went into the bedroom to change clothes. His dark suit was of the latest cut, his shirt an immaculate white. He put the documents he'd composed in a leather case, donned his hat and overcoat, and walked out the door to meet Henri at Maspero's.

The younger man was pacing outside the restaurant door when Alcide arrive.

"I've never been anywhere this elegant," he confessed.

"Nothing to fear, Henri. Just follow me."

The two men were seated and placed orders for beef steaks, potatoes Dauphinois, and pumpkin pie for dessert. Once the waiter walked away, Alcide put his document case on the table.

"I have a business proposition for you. If my brother Antoine, your father, had lived, the Devereaux plantation would have been his. My own children are grown and gone to their own lives. In this case are documents we can finalize tomorrow at the Cabildo if you agree. The first makes you my ward. Now, I know you're of age, but I need that to make you heir to what would have been your father's once I'm gone. The other is an offer to operate the plantation under my supervision until such time as I am no longer needed that role."

Henri was rendered speechless, but only temporarily.

"I never expected ..."

"I know." Alcide smiled. "I would like you to consider moving into the Rampart Street house as well. If that would suit."

"I don't know what to say."

"Start with yes or no; until you say one of those words, we cannot do anything else."

"Yes, sir. Very much yes." Henri extended his hand across the table and Alcide shook it.

The waiter brought their meals and Alcide requested a good bottle of red wine to toast then new partnership with his nephew."

"Merry Christmas, Henri."

"Merry Christmas, uncle. And thank you."

The Railroad

Christmas, 1875
Chicago

"Grandpappy, you should rest. You all worked so hard to put this feast together." The young girl's voice was serious.

"No, ma'am. I need to tell you this-here story. You got no idea what it was like. Even now, things bad as they are, you got no idea what it was like for us then. I got to tell you about the River Man and the railroad. 'T'weren't for that River Man, we wouldn't be havin' a feast like this-here."

"That doesn't make any sense, Grandpappy. River men are on boats, not railways." The girl's voice and words showed her confusion.

"This River Man is why your grandmammy, grandpappy, and your mammy got North so you could be born in freedom. Here's how it happened.

"Your grandmammy and me was slaves on the Delatoire place, out along the River Road. Now, that's a beautiful place, and I hope one day you get to see it. Why, this time of year the levees was all lit up with bonfires, each place doin' their own fancy wood stackin' to make the fires take a partic'lar shape. Mm, mm. It was a sight to see.

"Anyways, Madame Marie Delatoire, she was what you might call a termagant, if you were bein' generous in your terminology. She was a mean woman. Her husband went away to war and come back in 1863 with one leg and half his mind missin', so she had to run the whole operation. She didn't care about keepin' safe during cane-cuttin' or any of that; she just wanted the work done, night nor day.

"Ol' Michie Jean Delatoire, he was a good man as masters went. So far as I know, he ain't never raped a slave the way his son did. That boy, Michie Artaud, he was a bad 'un. Half the gals on the place who had big bellies had 'em from the young michie. Ol' Michie, he ain't stop his boy from doin' what he did. Weren't too many tears shed in the quarters when we learned young Michie got hisself killed in the war. If you was to ask me, I'd say the young michie's death was what made Ol' Michie Jean lose half his mind.

"This here tale is gettin' away from me, so I got to back up some.

"It was Ol' Michie Jean who let your grandmammy and me jump the broom. See, slaves weren't allowed to have no legal wedding with a minister and a bible and all that. We just jumped the broom and set up housekeeping. Couldn't have no legal wedding because the michies and madames had the right to sell us up or down the river at any time. Only protection anyone had was the children; if they was under eight years old, they couldn't be sold away from their mammies. Leastwise, that's what the law said. I know for a fact that it didn't always go that way.

"Your grandmammy, Tee Anne, she was the prettiest little woman I'd ever seen. There was already a Gros Anne ... big Anne ... so your grandmammy was little Anne. You know she's pretty now, but you should have seen her when she was a young woman. Walkin' through the yard, her nose in the air because she know she's a fine-lookin' gal. Reckon everyone was surprised when a house maid like her fell in love with a dark man like your grandpappy Hubert. But she done set her cap for me, and I fell in love with her hard. So, we went to Michie Jean and asked could we jump the broom. He said yes, and assigned us our own half a cabin to share. In those days, there were two rooms to a cabin, and each family had one of them rooms to themselves.

"By and by, your grandmammy's belly got big. That baby turned out to be your mammy. Madame Marie named the baby Louise. See, that's another thing. We weren't allowed name our own babies. Reckon the michies and madames was afraid we'd give 'em names from Senegal, or Gambia, or the Congo ... places our grandparents and parents was stolen from. That ain't allowed, no way. Anyway, Madame Marie wrote down your mammy's name in her record book, along with my name and Tee Anne's, to show that baby was born a slave. In them days, babies had the status of their mammies. If'n the mammy was a slave, the baby was too.

"I reckon it was so them babies made by the young michies on the black gals couldn't be free ... but maybe that's just me talkin'. Don't rightly know why that partic'lar law got made.

"Well, one day Madame Marie takes it into her head that Ol' Michie Jean got a fancy for Tee Anne. She sees her husband talkin' to the maid, speakin' soft and low. He was talkin' to Tee Anne about teachin' her and little Louise how to read which, you might know, was against the law in them days. By this time, Louise's about five years old. Ain't never been no more children for the Delatoires, and I think Ol' Michie Jean was lonely to have some little ones around him. Ain't gonna be no grandchildren neither, so that may account for how fond he got of Louise.

"So, Madame Marie starts talkin' loud and long, where Tee Anne can hear, that she's gonna sell Tee Anne and Louise up the river to Natchez-Under-the-Hill. Now, in them days Natchez had a big ol' slave market. This was no secret. What wasn't talked about so much is how many of our black gals got sold to madames in them bawdy houses.

"So, by and by, Tee Anne and me start plannin' on runnin' away. We figure it'll be worth the risk, because maybe we can get free of this whole mess. Heard many a time from loaned-out slaves about a bunch of folks as helps you get North, so we start puttin' out feelers via them slaves.

"That's how we learned about this fellow everyone calls River Man. He's a conductor on what they called the Underground Railroad. He takes people to the next conductor up the road, a fellow in New Orleans they call the Man from Paris. None of these conductors use their real names; they's in violation of the Fugitive Slave Act, and could be killed for what they're doin'. So, they were takin' a real risk to help us out.

"Through this and that kind of way, we get word to the River Man and he say he'll meet us in a partic'lar place on a partic'lar night. So, we steal off in the night and make it to the oak where he says to meet him. He's an older man, wearin' an old, beat-up hat with a red turkey feather in it. That means he was the toughest man on his boat. He got muscles, hard eyes, and a strip of black material 'round his arm says that he lost someone he loved. He looks like a mean ol' swamp rat, but then he speaks and you could tell that no matter how hard he tries to cover it, he's an educated Creole man.

"He's got a scrawny ol' mule, and a cart filled with junk. That cart got a false bottom; your mammy, Tee Anne and me, we all squeeze in under there. It's an uncomfortable ride to New Orleans, that's for sure. But the River Man, he get us there. We get out in the courtyard of a house, and a black man, who says he's the Man from Paris, hid us in his basement until the next conductor come and got us.

"Now, I'm pretty sure I heard that Man from Paris call the River Man Alcide ... which makes me wonder if he ain't Ol' Michie Devereaux. He freed his own plantation's people long before that damn war ever happened, practic'ly the minute he inherited the place. I didn't ask no questions, though; I figure can't no one beat out of me what I don't know. And if I'm right, I sure as the devil ain't gonna give him away no how.

"So, by and by, we all get here to Illinois. That's the state where that good man Mister Lincoln was from. We reckon that's a good place to put down our roots and so we do.

"So, while we're bowin' our heads thankin' Jesus for comin' this time of the year, we also need to be thankin' Him for the River Man and the Railroad."

A Light Across the Lake

Nous Sommes Deux Heures

2 *:00 AM*
   Paris

Lucien Dubois was always glad when the ormolu clock set in the fireplace at his end of the Opera Garnier's Grand Foyer rang the two o'clock hour. It meant that the patrons and their parties were long gone and that he could remove his wig and livery. His work was far from over, though. There was the floor to sweep and the ashes to be cleared away so that a fresh fire could be laid before the next performance.

Lucien enjoyed serving in the Grand Foyer; it gave him a chance to hear the well-to-do folk talk about the sets he had helped build. Servants were treated as though they were invisible, but no one knew his name anyway.

At twenty years of age, Lucien was also one of the senior apprentices in the set shop; he was a gifted woodworker already, specializing in the miniatures used to create a set. He sometimes joked that it was in his blood; Dubois literally translated to "of the forest."

Usually, Lucien finished his duties in the Grand Foyer and then went back to the dormitories where he lived with his fellow apprentices. Tonight, he had other plans.

Lucien had heard rumors of an actual house in one of the lower cellars of the opera house. Tonight, after all of the chandeliers were dark and the fireplaces empty, he planned to find out the truth of the matter.

If it is true, I will use the house-within-a-house design in a set model someday. If it is not true, at least I will know for certain.

Sunday was Lucien's one day off for the week. No one cared how late he slept, or where he went. Sometimes, he would go to mass with his family; they all favored the priest at Saint Sulpice. Sometimes, he read a book. Sometimes he walked around the beautiful city that he called home. In these ways, he was like most of the other apprentices.

What set him apart from his fellows, more than anything else, was his nearly insatiable curiosity.

Off came the white gloves; it was time for the dirty work. The metal ash bucket felt heavier than usual, simply because Lucien was in a hurry to be done with his sweeping and cleaning. The refuse was hauled out to the heap, where the ash would be wetted down to make lye for soap and the trash carried away by the rag and junk man.

Lucien was proud of his work, even in the steward's serving role. He was able to give money to his family, and the hard work made his body strong. The women of the costume shop had remarked on his handsome face, dark curls, and deep blue eyes more than once and always loudly enough for him to hear. He was tall and well-built.

Despite the attentions of the seamstresses, Lucien kept largely to himself. He preferred the opera's library, with its collection of set models right alongside the books, to carousing with his fellow apprentices. Lucien had dreams of becoming known for his designs, and thus spent what little spare time he had in study.

Lucien was one of the few apprentices who did not spend his money in the cribs of Place Pigalle. Not that he was priggish; he knew his funds were needed at home and could not see the point of wasting money on whores and absinthe. That was not to say that he had no dreams of romance. Lucien had fancied himself in love a few times. There had been the chorine who enjoyed his company until she found a wealthy "sponsor" amongst the opera's male patrons. And there had been a scullery maid who eventually went back to her home in the country, saying the city was "too fast" for her.

And how his fellow apprentices teased him over his fondness for the dark-haired equestrienne who rode the big black mare! He loved watching her practice; the horse seemed to float across the ground with no visible command from the woman on her back.

Lucien knew her name: Claire Delacroix. It had appeared in many a program at the opera house. He also knew that, for a long time, she had been very sad. Lately, there was more light in her eyes and in her step. She did not seem the sort to take a sponsor, so Lucien decided that she must be in love.

She had been in the Grand Foyer that evening, dressed in a blue ball gown trimmed with fine black lace, enjoying a drink during the entr'acte. Sapphires sparkled at her ears and in her hair; a heavy collar of the blue stones wrapped around her throat and cascaded down her bosom.

"You look beautiful this evening, Mademoiselle," Lucien said as he took her empty champagne glass.

"Thank you, Monsieur ..."

"Dubois. Lucien Dubois." He bowed over her hand, wishing that he were wearing anything but the absurd, old-fashioned livery and wig.

"Monsieur Dubois," she smiled and nodded, then left the Grand Foyer. He wished that he knew where she was sitting, imagining himself inviting her for something to eat after the performance.

But that was pure fantasy; he had to put her from his mind. Besides, up close he could tell that she was at least ten years older than himself. He had nothing to offer her.

Maybe she had a sponsor after all; how else would she have such jewels? Working in the set shop meant he could tell paste when he saw it, and those were no fakes borrowed from the costumers. These jewels were costly gifts from a patron.

She is not for you, Lucien.

He returned to his dormitory to change clothes. Tonight's plans called for simple brogans, cord trousers, and a rough shirt. He donned his laborer's attire, collected a lantern, and went to the library to look at Charles Garnier's plans for the building. The drawings showed him all of the connections he needed to make to plumb the lowest depths of the building: the fifth cellar. The only part of the building he'd never explored.

Down stairwells and hallways he went, his lantern lighting the way in the darkness. The quiet was disconcerting; the usual bustle of the busy opera house was absent in the wee hours.

After what seemed an eternity, Lucien reached his destination, only to find a lake. Engineers had never successfully drained the fifth cellar, despite their efforts. Lucien shone his light on the water and watched a sleek shape glide past. Dear God, a sturgeon, of all things! There had to be a stream coming in from the Seine somewhere.

He lifted the lantern and peered into the distance. He saw lights across the way; surely that was more than mere reflection! There was only one way to find out. He took off his shoes and stockings; they remained behind with the lantern as he entered the cold water.

Lucien was a strong swimmer, but the lights ahead were further away than he'd thought. A quick look back toward his lantern showed that he was about halfway; turning back would take just as long as moving forward.

The water was much colder than he had anticipated, and every now and again a fish – the same sturgeon, perhaps – bumped into him.

He kept swimming.

❧ ☙

A bell chimed in the distance; the signal had not rung its alert in a long time. Erik LeMaître kissed Claire one more time – would he ever feel sated where her lips were concerned? – and got out of bed.

"What is it?" Claire murmured as she sat up, pulling the coverlet over herself. She wore nothing but the sapphire necklace.

"There's something outside, and I don't think it's that sturgeon." Her lover drew on his trousers and slipped a mask over his face.

Claire reached for Erik's discarded shirt and pulled it over her head. She got out of bed and followed him out of his underground home and into the cavernous cellar.

"God in heaven!" she exclaimed as Erik turned an unconscious body over on the walkway. "It's Lucien Dubois, the steward from the Grand Foyer."

"Yes, and also one of the set shop apprentices." Erik peered into the distance, seeing a speck of light. "The idiot swam here! I'll take the gondola to bring back his lantern before a rat upsets it and burns the whole place to the ground." His tone was one of disgust.

Claire, in the meanwhile, was examining Lucien as though he were one of her horses.

"He's chilled to the bone," she said. "Look at his skin; it's almost blue."

Erik rolled his eyes and picked up the unconscious youth as easily as though he were an infant. "You start the caldarium, my love. I'll bring the lost sheep so that you can warm him."

Erik pretended more impatience with Claire's compassion than he felt, and both of them knew it. Claire smiled and ran ahead to the deep stone basin to open the tap.

Erik deposited the shivering, unconscious youth on the top step of the caldarium. "You'll have to get him out of these foul clothes. I'll be back soon to help you with him."

"Lucien, you foolish boy," Claire murmured. "What on earth were you thinking?"

Practicality was the order of the day; she used a pair of shears to cut the shirt and trousers at the seams as the hot water filled the tub around her. Erik's linen shirt clung to her uncorseted curves.

Claire was quick and efficient in her work; before long, Lucien wore nothing but his pants and was coming to as the hot water rose around him, his eyes rolling a bit.

"Slip down one more step, Lucien. No, no. Don't stand. Just slip down. There you are."

Claire sat on the step Lucien had just vacated, her arm around the boy's shoulders. She spoke to him in the same tones she used with an injured or frightened animal.

"What ... where?" Lucien's eyelids fluttered again.

"Just stay where you are; you're chilled to the bone."

"Mademoiselle Delacroix?" His quiet question showed his confusion. "How?"

"Never you mind what, where, or how, Lucien Dubois."

"My clothes!" His awareness was returning.

"Never mind those as well," Claire replied. "They were ruined by your swim."

"They would be, I suppose." He groaned. "I don't suppose I could have some soap?" He was suddenly conscious of how he might smell.

"Of course." Claire got out of the tub and retrieved a cake of Erik's sandalwood soap. Lucien gaped as he realized how little she wore.

"I'm sorry," she said as she handed him the soap. "I was more worried about warming you than about dressing myself. And I'm not leaving you alone."

"There is no need, my love." Erik had returned, holding an extinguished lantern and Lucien's heavy shoes. "Please, go change into something dry. I will watch our intruder."

Lucien had never seen anything like Erik LeMaître's face. When he took off the mask, the skin under it was discolored ... a reddish-purple birthmark stained thin skin, one eyelid was nearly gone, and the nare on that side of his nose completely so. Scars that could only have come from a stinging lash covered his back. He stepped out of his trousers and into the tub.

"Go ahead and wash up, boy. And stop gawping like a fish. If you slip under the water and drown, Claire will never forgive me."

When Claire returned, clad in riding breeches, boots, and a shirt, Lucien's teeth were no longer chattering. Color had returned to his face and lips, and he was responding in a rather lively fashion to Erik's pointed questions about his early morning swim.

"What you have here is amazing," he was saying. "I must incorporate into a set design."

"Lucien," Claire said quietly, "that is exactly what you must not do. Neither Erik nor I would be safe."

The youth started to protest, but fell silent. He gave Claire a beseeching look and spoke at last.

"He's your patron, isn't he?" Lucien's tone was glum.

"No, he isn't. He's my lover, certainly, but I am not ..."

"She's a lady," Erik interrupted, his voice like ice, as Claire walked away. "Her circumstances are reduced. That is all."

He got out of the tub and reached for a nearby towel.

"Dry off and follow me." His tone brooked no resistance and Lucien obeyed.

In the main part of Erik's home, Claire waited with hot tea and cold beef sandwiches. When the two men reappeared, Lucien was wearing one of Erik's nightshirts. He fell on the repast gratefully.

"Might I have another cup of tea?" he asked.

"Of course," Erik replied, taking the youth's cup and saucer. With his back to Lucien, he tipped a small vial of powder into the hot tea. Claire saw what Erik and done and nodded her acknowledgment.

They didn't have to wait long for the drug to take effect. Once Lucien was sound asleep, Erik slung the youth over his shoulder like a sack of potatoes. With Claire carrying the lantern, they made their way back to the opera house dormitories by way of the Communard road.

Nous Sommes Quatorze Heures

2:00 PM

Paris

Lucien Dubois awoke in his own bed. He wore a nightshirt of fine linen instead of his usual red wool flannel. On the bench at the foot of his bed rested his shoes, cleaned and polished, and a shirt and trousers of better quality than any he had ever owned.

On top of the clothes was a sealed letter; the deckled edge was the black of mourning stationery.

His head muzzy, Lucien reached for the letter and broke the red wax seal. The handwriting inside was spidery and almost childlike.

"Monsieur Dubois,

"I hope you will accept these replacements for the garments that were damaged by your foolish exploits.

"When you return to the scenery shop tomorrow, you will find that you have been promoted to journeyman.

"Your skills are such that you have long deserved this. However, the price of this promotion is your silence. Should I learn that you have bruited certain information around the opera house, I cannot but feel sorry for you ... and the family that needs your income."

There was no signature, but Lucien had no doubt of who had written it.

The black-edged letters were infamous in the opera house; Lucien had been in the presence of the so-called Opera Ghost himself! He thought back to the scarred body of the man who had – there was no denying it – saved his life. The man who was Claire Delacroix's lover.

Lucien could still smell the sandalwood soap on his skin, as well as the lavender that had been kept in the clothespress with the nightshirt he wore.

Even if he did decide to tell someone, who would believe him? Everyone told tales of the Opera Ghost and his mysterious notes –

and just about everyone thought them silly phantasmagorias good for nothing but frightening the chorines.

Lucien put the note on the highest shelf of his own clothespress, far out of sight. No one could know of it. He folded the nightshirt, resolving to put lavender in with his own garments so that they would carry the sophisticated scent, and donned the new clothing.

On his way out of the opera house yard to visit his family for church, and to tell them of his good fortune, he passed Claire Delacroix. She was riding her Friesian mare, Josephine; they had just come from a brief turn around the nearby Parc Monceau.

"Bonjour, Mademoiselle Delacroix!" He turned on his heel, tipped his cap, and then took the horse's reins so that Claire could dismount.

Lucien's gaze was frank and admiring; Claire wore a green and black riding habit that suited her perfectly. The gleaming black sidesaddle from which she extricated herself could only have come from Hermes. Claire's lover was a generous, and fortunate, man.

"I want to thank you," he began, only to be stopped by a black-gloved finger laid gently across his lips.

"No thanks are necessary."

"But ..."

She held up her hand. "I know what has been done for you, and what was asked of you in return. Keep your end of the bargain, mon ami."

She reclaimed Josephine's reins and walked toward the stables without a backward glance.

Lucien watched her go, a slightly wistful smile crossing his face. Then, he turned toward Saint Sulpice, and home.

Two Days in June

5 *June 1832*

Enjolras kissed his pretty Marianne goodbye and pulled on his trousers.

"I'll be back with supper," he said, as she pulled the blankets over herself.

"After your meeting, of course." Even her pout was adorable.

"Yes, chérie, after the meeting."

"Bring that useless Grantaire with you," Marianne called after him. "Otherwise, I'll never hear the end of it from Olympe."

❧ ☙

General Jean Maximilien Lamarque was dead, taken by the cholera. He'd died in the old hospital; Lariboisiere had not yet been built when the epidemic hit. You may know that hospital; it is still in use today. It is in the 10th arrondissement, although they didn't call it that at the time.

Henri Grantaire could scarcely credit it; it seemed that Lamarque would go on forever. So much larger than life he'd been; hell, Grantaire had served under him in '30, right next to Jean-Claude Enjolras. Little they'd all known; even Lamarque had said they'd been in the wrong, putting Louis-Philippe on the throne.

Grantaire's feet dragged along the rue Saint-Denis to the tavern. He'd agreed to meet Enjolras there, as well as some of their fellow students from the Sorbonne. How old Grantaire felt when he considered the youthful enthusiasms of Bahorel, Combeferre, Courfeyrac, Feuilly, Joly: all of them were children in his eyes — even the well-spoken Jean Prouvaire, with his idealism. The eldest of the group, Lesgle, was a duke's heir; the entire lot was vehemently anti-royalist. Really, it was their only common bond.

❧ ☙

They called themselves the Friends of the Abaissé, an adjunct of the Society of the Rights of Man. To Grantaire's cynical eyes, they were just another Sorbonne fraternity: wealthy young men playing at philosophy and high-flown ideals of revolution and war without having the slightest idea of the true cost of either. Each time they agreed to meet at the ABC Tavern ("I'll see you at the Abaissé"), they reveled in their own cleverness at making a pun.

If Combeferre was the group's guide and Courfeyrac its center, as they'd all often opined, Enjolras was its Chief. When the other men spoke of their mistresses, Enjolras claimed that la Patrie — the Republic — was his only woman.

Of course, Grantaire thought that was another glorious pun. Enjolras' love was the plump, delightful Marianne, whose parents had named her for the spirit of the Republic. She shared a flat with Olympe, who had nearly as much a hold on Grantaire as his beloved wine.

Wine. Yes, he needed more wine. Perhaps a lengthy toast to the people's general would be in order once he got to the tavern.

❧ ❧

Bahorel bought another round of wine for the group; it was his turn, after all. At least Grantaire was late; that meant the bottle would last longer. The veteran-student was always drowning his sorrows.

Combeferre and Feuilly were playing dice, while Courfeyrac and Prouvaire loudly debated a point of philosophy. It looked to be just one more night in the dingy tavern on the rue de la Chanverrie.

Until Grantaire entered, his face solemn as a judge, followed by an equally subdued Enjolras.

Grantaire picked up the nearest glass — which happened to be Bahorel's.

"A toast to fallen comrades, my friends," he intoned. "General Lamarque has gone to his reward."

❧ ❧

Before we learn more about our friends on this particular evening, first we must know about how they arrived at this place. Grantaire and

Enjolras are the elder statesmen, although not the eldest of the group. They are the seasoned veterans ... the ones who fought under Lamarque just two years previously to put Louis-Philippe on the throne. At the time, they believed in their cause.

But now, that Louis has proved as dissolute as many others of the same name. The people of Paris are starving; there are no animals to be seen, as pets and zoo animals alike have been eaten. The same thing happened during the Reign of Terror; starvation kills ethics just as surely as it kills the hungry. Crime increases when people grow more desperate.

And Louis-Philippe does nothing to help the hungry.

Grantaire and Enjolras discuss these problems frequently during their visits to Marianne and Olympe ... to the disgust of the young women, who would like their beaux's attention to be undivided. Unlike the monarch, the two men cannot look upon suffering and remain silent. And so, they began to talk of revolution.

❧ ☙

Let us first look to Henri Grantaire. He and Enjolras have known one another since childhood, after all, and are nearly as close as brothers.

But do not presume they were equals in the nursery. On the contrary, young Henri was the son of the majordomo. His father served the Enjolras household.

Henri was a quick boy, but not always quick enough. His father was swift with physical punishment, most particularly when he though the boy was putting on airs above his station.

And how might the little Grantaire be doing this? Why, by befriending the solitary Jean-Claude, scion of the bourgeois household that gave the elder Grantaire his living.

Henri had noticed the solemn boy, who seemed to be near his own age. A shy offer to pet a precious dog on the young master's part soon led to sharing Henri's rolling hoop, the two boys running after it. Their laughter echoed across the lawn, with a joyful dog barking counterpoint and nipping at their heels.

Jean-Claude begged his father to allow his new friend to sit in the nursery during sessions with the tutor. Thus, the butler's boy and the gentleman's son had identical educations.

For his part, Grantaire was always the more grounded of the two. He had an eye toward the practical. He saw life in all its ugly reality.

It is no wonder that he took to drink at a relatively early age. Wine and brandy dulled all manner of pain, whether from the bitter reality that he would never be more than a servant's son to the physical pain of his father's fists landing yet another blow.

Perhaps you are thinking that Grantaire's father should have been grateful for the generosity shown to his son. However, you must also remember that pride is a very peculiar thing. A man does not always like the idea of his son surpassing him on the world's stage. Such a son might look down on his father.

And so it was that the elder Grantaire determined to keep young Henri humble, by any means necessary.

It did not help that Henri looked so much like the mother who died giving him life. Fair-haired and blue-eyed, the lad had been the recipient of the scullery maids' sidelong glances since his days in short pants.

For contrast, look upon the dreamer, Jean-Claude Enjolras. As dark as his young friend is fair, this lad prefers his books and his dog to rowdier sport. It is because of this that his father, a well-to-do draper, encourages his friendship with the less-polished Grantaire boy. Life must be lived, not dreamed about in a classroom.

So it is that the unlikely pair become the very best of friends and are soon inseparable. Each of us has had just such a childhood friend; even when the slings and arrows of life move us apart for a time, we always come back like metal to a lodestone. So it was with Grantaire and Enjolras.

As they got older, their antics grew apace. Grantaire it was who took Enjolras to a Montmartre crib for his first encounter with a whore. Grantaire had, by that time, had nearly every scullery maid belowstairs. At least one had been dismissed with a big belly and no reference.

Enjolras was delighted by the pleasures of the flesh, to be sure, but could never hope to be his friend's equal in debauchery. This young Enjolras, it must be said, saw himself as destined for greater things.

The boys' tutor was wont to complain that young Jean-Claude had his head more frequently in the clouds than in his lesson books. Yet, each assignment was completed, on-time and correctly. The schoolmaster deemed it a puzzle.

Enjolras steeped himself in history books; deeds and exploits of the past were his true religion, no matter how many times he attended mass in the family chapel.

It was in this vein that, his head filled to the brim with heroes, Enjolras went to war at the tender age of eighteen. Grantaire, not to be left out of drinking, wenching and fighting were in the offing, followed suit.

Two years on, this same Grantaire and Enjolras study at the Sorbonne. Enjolras reads the law and Grantaire philosophy. They have seen more of life than their fellow students .. far more than they wanted to see. Grantaire most often views life through the distortions of a wine bottle as he tries to forget the fetid stench of the battlefields.

As for Jean-Claude Enjolras, he puts on his elegant suit of clothes and goes through his day. What cannot readily be seen is the fervor for justice and equality that burn in his heart. Each tale of his country's revolutions has made him determined to see better times for all his countrymen.

It is this same belief in equality that saw him offer to let the butler's son pet his beloved dog.

As I said, there are seldom any cats or dogs to be seen nowadays. As with the zoo animals in 1789, there has been too much hunger in the streets. The starving cannot afford to be sentimental over pets.

And so it is that Enjolras' soul is aflame with a fanatic desire that none should know hunger or want. The child of privilege has seen far too much of both, between the pages of his books and on the battlegrounds.

So, too, one General Jean Maximilien Lamarque had seen too much. When Louis-Philippe could not be bothered to keep his promises to France, Lamarque spoke out. Once a supporter, Lamarque became an outspoken critic of the crown.

And of what did he speak? Lack of meaningful work. Lack of homes. Lack of food.

And what did the well-to-do of Paris say to this lack?

Nothing.

To Enjolras' view, it was almost as bad as Marie-Antoinette's legendary, albeit inaccurately quoted, let them eat cake.

There was no cake, and little bread, to be had. An income from Enjolras père kept clothes on the younger man's back and a roof over his head.

And Grantaire? Each month's modest pension from the king's army bought a garret room and cheap drink.

How, then, do these youths have mistresses like Marianne and Olympe — beautiful young women who might easily seek wealthier company?

Both girls sew for a dressmaker. They are fortunate that the lighting is good and the hours fair for the wage given. Not all are so fortunate.

Olympe's own mother, after all, had sold herself to make ends meet after the child's father abandoned them.

All too common a tale in this place and time.

And where did these four meet?

In the gathered crowd during one of Lamarque's speeches. The moment Marianne's blue eyes fell on Enjolras, she declared herself smitten, and nothing would do but that she must sidle closer while dragging Olympe in her wake.

From that moment, Grantaire declared himself Olympe's slave. She returned his regard joyously.

Many a night saw the four of them together, dining in the women's rooms before retiring to their respective bedchambers.

Each night, after their lovemaking, Marianne prayed that Jean-Claude would ask for her hand. Being a lawyer's wife was a step up for a grocer's daughter.

Each night, that same Enjolras would talk of France's future — but never his own, with or without Marianne.

It seemed that he could only envision the former.

Olympe doesn't worry so much about a future with Grantaire. She worries more about getting through until tomorrow. This is her mother's legacy. Her father left no legacy, of course. Perhaps this is why Olympe takes such an epicurean view of her lover, and of her life.

And so, these are the major players upon our little stage. And what, you may well ask, does our stage look like?

The winding, narrow streets of the Latin Quarter inform our tale. The cat's-head cobblestones lead to stone buildings, some elegant dwellings and some mere tenements. The students live in the latter, for the most part; even Baron Pontmercy's heir has humble rooms, so that his fellow students will not know him for an aristo.

But this is not young Pontmercy's tale, and so we will leave him there.

As we have already observed, there are no pets left in Paris; there is, however, another kind of animal. There are droves of hungry children, the grubby little gamines whose parents send them out to beg for a crust of bread .. if they have parents at all. Many of them are expert cutpurses and pickpockets, melting into the dank, narrow alleys with the booty taken from unsuspecting passersby.

As with any large city, the backstreets are filled with whores and mountebanks, wigmakers buying desperate women's hair, dentists buying anyone's teeth .. in short, the usual sorts who prey on those most in need of kindness.

At least the wigmaker and dentist give coin instead of taking it.

There are also the priests of nearby Notre Dame, providing a bowl of soup and small loaf of bread to each hungry Parisian who stands in line, until the provisions run out.

And so the stage is set, and our actors gathered.

But wait: there is first one more person with whom we must be acquainted. That is Robert Enjolras, second son of that aforementioned family. Though Napoleon's law says that all children inherit equally, there are still some who hold to older ways. Thus it is that this same Robert goes for a soldier. Had there been a third son, he would have been for the church; however, Divine Providence has seen fit to send only Jean-Claude and Robert to Monsieur and Madame Enjolras.

So, young Robert moves through the ranks swiftly, riding the back of a bought commission. At the time of our tale, he is a captain of the National Guard, every bit as passionate and handsome as his elder brother.

And now, my friends, let us return to the tavern. Young men with old souls are plotting!

❦

"A toast to fallen comrades, my friends. General Lamarque has gone to his reward."

Grantaire drains Bahorel's glass and smacks his lips in satisfaction as he returns it to his dismayed companion.

"What do you know of the funeral plans?" Combeferre inquires. "Surely there will be a procession, with catafalque and all."

"Indeed," Feuilly joins in. "The people of Paris will want to pay their respects."

"We must find out." Enjolras speaks with authority. "For we may well use this somber occasion to make a change for the better, all over France."

Grantaire sees the familiar light in his friend's eye and shakes his head.

"Innkeeper," he calls out genially. "More of your wine, and good meat pies, for all. Plotting has ever been hungry work."

With that, he throws some coins on the table. The innkeeper's daughter snatches them up when she brings the requested items, barely acknowledging Grantaire as she slaps greasy trays on tables.

And so it is that the night wears on, in discussion of weapons, gunpowder and treason. Revolution has ever been thus.

⋅≼ ≽⋅

Of all of those clear-eyed idealists, Grantaire is the one with a secret: he wishes he were a father. Where others of his number might give a cuff and a "Be gone with you, brat!" to the filthy gamines who steal to stave off starvation, Grantaire is the one who shares his bread. Grantaire is the one who provides a penny here and there, though he has little enough himself.

Though he has never known serious need, he has known what it is to look upon those who have more and to feel the pain of lack.

But for the grace of God, thinks he, I could be one of those ravening little boys eking out their living on the streets by any means necessary.

Grantaire thinks, from time to time, of marrying Olympe .. or of throwing both caution and precaution to the winds and getting a child on her. Either scenario will cause her to lose her situation with the dressmaker, though. And, in times such as these, perhaps it is best not to bring another babe into the world. There are mouths enough already crying for food. Thus, this particular desire remains unspoken.

Grantaire wonders whether he truly recalls hearing a story of a man jailed for stealing bread .. or if it was an illusion found in the bottom of a wine bottle.

He shakes his head to clear it and heads out into the night, handing a coin to a lad of about six years in age and 60 in countenance and demeanor. He is around the tavern nearly as much as the students.

"It is late for you to be about, little Gavroche," Grantaire tells the boy. "Go buy your bread and cheese, and hide away safely."

"My thanks, monsieur," the boy replies. "This will feed me and the other two boys I'm helping. My babies and I thank you."

With that, the gamine melts into the darkness of the Saint-Michel slums as Grantaire makes his way homeward.

For his part, Enjolras goes neither to his home nor the waiting arms of Marianne. Instead, he makes his way to a certain army barracks. There he speaks with the handsome young captain he calls brother and learns of the plans for Lamarque's funeral procession. Now he knows the route, the hour .. all.

He also knows that Robert will be amongst the honor guard.

Whether this is an ill omen or good, only Divine Providence will tell.

Enjolras arises from Marianne's bed far earlier than either of them desire. His bodily needs have been slaked; neither of them knows of a certainty what the day will bring, and it may well be their last time together.

The guns have been hidden in the tavern; today they will be unpacked and handed to men who, except for Enjolras and Grantaire, have never shot at anything other than game animals .. if even that.

"May God have mercy on all of their souls," prays Jean-Claude Enjolras, as he prepares to lead men into battle once again.

5 JULY 1832

Has it really been only thirty days? Marianne asks herself.

Thirty days since 300 Republicans, led by Enjolras, stopped Lamarque's funeral in the Place de la Bastille? How well she remembers the day, and her lover's rousing speeches to the gathered crowd. It seemed that the people of Paris would follow Jean-Claude Enjolras to the mouth of Hell itself. After all, they applauded every phrase that came from his mouth and the mouths of the others who spoke on Lamarque's very catafalque.

And yet, that is not what happened at all, is it?

The people, at the end of the day, stayed home."

The Friends of the Abaissé, along with their newfound comrades, barricaded the narrow streets around Place de la Bastille, and they waited for the people to come.

And they waited.

The only ones who came were the National Guard, twenty-thousand strong on the first day. Among them was one Robert Enjolras who, though sympathetic to his brother, was not sympathetic to the Republican cause. He was sorry he had ever told Jean-Claude the route that Lamarque's funeral cortège would take.

The first night, Marianne took a basket of food to Enjolras for him to share amongst his comrades behind the barricades. The meat, cheese, and wine disappeared so quickly! Hunger was a motivator for many behind the lines that evening. Once the food was shared around, Marianne begged Jean-Claude to come home with her, but he was steadfast.

"The people will come, ma petite, I am sure of it."

He would not be moved, and so Marianne went back to her little room to keep vigil.

Olympe reported a similar failure with Grantaire; she had brought him a bottle of cognac and the promise of a night of debauchery. None of that mattered to him ... for once.

And now, here they were, just a little more than a week before the Fête de la Fédération ... alone.

On that second day, the National Guard sent 20,000 more men than they had the day before. So, facing the Friends of the Abaissé and their few comrades were 40,000 well-trained, well-fed soldiers.

No one knows for certain which side fired the first shot. Not even the very nice Monsieur Hugo, whose wife was a client at the dressmaker; he had been caught behind one of the barricades and felt that his escape had been narrow indeed. He planned, he said, to write a book about the matter one day.

But, Marianne thought, it does not matter who fired first. At the end of that second June day, 93 of the Republicans and 30 of the soldiers lay dead ... among them both Enjolras sons and one Henri Grantaire. The bodies were laid out in long ranks, and both Marianne and Olympe had screamed at the sight of their lovers there. This was the one outcome that none of them had foreseen.

Of the Friends of the Abaissé, only young Pontmercy survives in person. The others survive only in spirit. While this is not his tale, it is Pontmercy who tells Marianne and Olympe what became of their lovers. Of how Grantaire was collapsed, drunk, inside a tavern during the entire battle. Of how, when the soldiers pushed Enjolras into the tavern at bayonet-point, to execute him for being the ringleader of the Republicans, Grantaire awoke at last.

Of how Grantaire arose with dignity, walked to the wall and stood next to his friend as the bullets flew.

The two men who were closer than brothers during life have gone into the next world together. Somehow, young Pontmercy opines, it is fitting.

The result of the whole thing is not what anyone would have predicted. Why? Because soon after those two days in June, the entire thing seems to have been forgotten. The people of Paris are still hungry, and the cruel king is still on the throne.

It has only been a bit more than 40 years since the first revolution, in 1789. Neither Marianne nor Olympe were yet born. Marianne remembers sitting by her grandmother's side, learning to sew with tiny, perfect stitches and listening to stories about the Jacobins, the Girondins, the Cordilleras, and so many other clubs whose names she has forgotten. Of how Grand-mère learned to make those tiny, perfect stitches after being conscripted, in the levée en masse of 1793 with all of the other Parisian women, to make tents and clothes. Of how Robespierre led a terror-filled time, until his life was taken by the same guillotine that had made the streets run red at his direction.

Somehow, she has never before connected that time to this. Never before has she considered that hunger and peoples' rights were the driving causes for both the uprisings of 1789 and the one that took Jean-Claude's life.

Never before has she considered that her charismatic lover was a Robespierre to the Friends of the Abaissé. Nor has she contemplated the similarities between those long-ago clubs and the gathering of Sorbonne students in a dark tavern, dreaming of a better world for all citizens.

And now she grows thoughtful. She wonders whether things will ever really get better for the people of her beloved city. And when the blood of those people will cease to stain the cat's-head cobblestones of Parisian streets.

The Friends of the Abaissé are, like the Girondins and the Jacobins, no more; it is as though they had never existed.

Except for two things.

In Marianne's heart there is now a spirit of rebellion: a belief that better days could and would come if people worked together. The old slogan of liberté, egalité, fraternité holds a very different meaning for her now, just a few days before the anniversary of the first French revolution, than it did during those days when Enjolras was her lover. Now it is a burning need to fight for the freedom of all.

And the other thing?

Grantaire's wish is coming true, if only he knew it. In Olympe's belly is his child.

Down on the Corner of Love

Down on the Corner of Love

When Jo Cooper introduced himself to me ("I'm Jo, no E."), he seemed like an elfin version of Oscar Wilde. His blonde curls hung in a riot around his face, and his pink ruffled shirt set off his coloring perfectly. He was barely taller than me, and chattered a mile a minute. We were in the basement laundry room of our San Francisco apartment building. My hair was tied back with a thick, purple hank of yarn that didn't quite match my sleeveless, mock turtleneck shell and coordinating pedal pushers. I was also wearing a horrible pale lipstick. Revlon's Silver City Pink, to be precise; a color that Jo says only looks good on the sisters. Against my pale skin, it was almost sickly. Fashionable, but sickly. I could almost hear Jo tut-tutting my outfit as he looked me up and down over the rims of his wire-framed granny glasses. Not that I blamed him.

Jo told me which apartment he lived in and asked if he could borrow some of my fabric softener. I handed over the jug, and he poured a capful into a washer full of colorful clothes.

As for me, I was swearing like a stevedore. Despite having consumed my quarters and dimes, the washer would not. Jo gave the recalcitrant machine a sharp kick and it began to fill.

Jo lived exactly one floor above me. We were both lucky enough to have units with bay windows overlooking Cole Street. Almost immediately, we started running back and forth to visit each other; it was as though we'd been friends forever.

I lived alone. My apartment had simple furnishings in far too many shades of beige. My closet was filled with A-line skirts and jumpers that I'd run up with yardage from Discount Fabrics and patterns by Butterick. Coordinating Peter Pan collar blouses and some rather matronly cardigans filled my work wardrobe; slacks and tops for weekends took up the other side of the closet. Jo said I needed much more color in my life.

My first visit to Jo's apartment was a revelation. There were cushions everywhere, and he used sari fabric that he bought in Berkeley for curtains. The entire place was a riot of color and comfort that stood in stark contrast to my own plain furnishings and ivory drapes. We'd sit on the floor, eating take-out Chinese food straight from the carton, and talk about books, movies, and music for hours. Every once in a while, Jo would pull out a pipe and we'd each take a hit or two. I loved spending time with him; every visit was like having a slumber party with your best gal-pal.

So, I wasn't really surprised when Jo confessed that he was gay. "I sleep with men," he said bluntly after passing me the pipe.

I thought back to my high school boyfriend's fumbling in the back of his family car while we were at the drive-in movies. "I do, too."

Jo thought it was hilarious.

Jo shared his apartment with a cat, a squalling Siamese named Pearl ("After Janis, you know?") who took to me at once.

"She doesn't like most people, Raine. You're one of the lucky ones."

That was another thing; he started calling me Raine almost immediately; Lorraine, he claimed, was the name of a stodgy old woman, and he just didn't see me that way.

Jo worked at the Sassoon salon on Union Square. I worked in a one-man law office for a Mr. Sterling. Our lives were very different from one another.

It was spring of 1967, and I was glad to have escaped my uptight Louisiana home for a more colorful place and time. I grew up in a tiny town called Eunice and went to secretarial school in Baton Rouge. My sister Pauline was pregnant again, even though her son Harmon wasn't even a year old, and my other sister Julie was being sweet-talked by some soldier. She'd be married and having babies soon herself. That was not the life I wanted. Sure, working for Mr. Sterling as a typist wasn't a glamorous job, but I could afford to do the things I wanted to most of the time and had a cute apartment. If I'd stayed in Eunice, that would never have happened.

A few weeks after our first meeting, Jo stopped by my apartment on his way upstairs after work. He wanted to invite me to join him for dinner at a new Chinese joint up on Haight. I came to the door wearing a hair dryer bonnet over enormous rollers, let him in, and then plugged the hose back into the plastic monstrosity. Luckily, my ears weren't under the bonnet, so we could hear ourselves talk.

"I can free you from that thing." Jo pointed at the rose-printed bubble covering my head. "I've got my scissors and stuff right here."

I turned off the dryer.

Jo cut my hair right in my kitchen. He grabbed a towel out of the bathroom and put it on the floor, planted a chair on top of it, and grabbed the dish towel from the oven handle. One hair clip from my big plastic rollers held the towel under my chin as scissors slashed and brown hair fell. First were the bangs, skimming my eyebrows. The rest seemed to take forever as Jo hemmed and hawed over what he wanted to do. When he was done, my hair was shorter than his! He picked up the towel, shook the hair into the kitchen trash, and pronounced himself pleased.

"No more awful rollers and goofy ponytails, Raine. Now, dear, where is your makeup?"

"On my dresser, in the bedroom."

"Most of this will never do," he said, coming out with the bag and sorting through it. "This awful frosty lipstick is going to be the first to hit the trash ... and this robin's egg blue eyeshadow won't be far behind. Let's go get dinner, and then we'll come back here."

Jo was as good as his word. After a dinner of mu shu pork and shrimp fried rice, he ransacked my makeup bag.

"Far too much Woolworth junk in here, sweetie. And we really need to talk about your clothes."

"What's wrong with them?" I was rather proud of my sewing.

"Your closet looks like it can't decide whether it belongs to a little girl or her granny, Raine. You're young and gorgeous; dress like it."

"I don't spend a lot of money for clothes, Jo. I make most of what I wear."

"There's nothing wrong with that on its own, Raine. It's just that you make these frumpy things." He held out a tan plaid jumper. "This is not the attire of a beautiful young woman."

Then he pulled a pair of jeans from the far back of my closet. They were fading, and I didn't wear them often.

"I'm taking these with me to L.A. over the weekend. I have a friend down there who will fix these right up." He wadded the jeans up and took them with him ... along with a bag full of the makeup he'd thrown away, just in case I was tempted to take it back.

When I went to work on Monday, Mr. Sterling, told me he liked my new haircut. He also told me he had a nephew he thought I should meet. I couldn't believe it. All I could imagine was a younger version of his short, bald self. I demurred and kept typing.

Besides, my sister Pauline had told me that I'd meet a curly-haired blonde man who was my soulmate. Surely she didn't mean Jo, although he was rapidly becoming my best friend. Pauline's visions were seldom wrong, and I was waiting to see what would happen with this one.

Jo came back from LA with my jeans and a ton of new records that he insisted on playing for me while we shared a pizza.

"My friend Diane painted them for you; she's got a little boutique on Melrose and one day she's going to be really big. She's doing stuff for Janis and Jimi."

Of course, I knew who they were. Janis Joplin was practically a neighbor, and we saw her all the time. I loved going to her shows; she was so full of energy. Plus, I must be honest; it was nice to hear a Southern voice besides my own now and again.

The pants were beautiful, with a design of flowers and butterflies on the lower legs.

"Now we just need to find you some tops," he said. "I picked one out from Diane's shop that I think you'll like."

The blouse had long bell sleeves, and a lot of embroidery. It was different from anything I'd ever owned.

"I don't know, Jo. I'm sure it was expensive. I'll have to pay you back in increments."

"It's a gift. And I know how to get good prices when I shop. Just you wait; I'll take you with me and you'll see."

Jo and I went out to hear music a lot. He seemed to know all the musicians. Besides Janis, there were all the people in Jefferson Airplane. They shared a huge, funky mansion over on Fillmore. Grace was one of the most beautiful women I'd ever seen and could sing like no one I'd ever heard.

I met a few fellows who seemed nice, but Jo always seemed to know things about them that made them less appealing. "He's looking for a sugar mama." "He's gay and looking for a beard." "I knew his last girlfriend, and he beat her up."

Some things weren't so different from Eunice, after all.

Mr. Sterling loosened up and started talking to me more. He turned out to be a really nice man, and while he went on about his nephew the doctor more than I liked to hear, he also talked about his wife. She had passed on a couple of years before, and I realized he was lonely. I wished he would meet some nice lady, but he was putting all his energy into keeping the business going. He handled wills and family law, so there weren't any criminals around or anything like that ... but just about everyone he met was a client.

"Janie and I weren't blessed with children," he confided one day. "I guess I feel like you're the daughter I never had. I hope that doesn't make me sound foolish."

I assured him that it didn't, and better understood why he was worried about my social life. There were so many things a single woman couldn't do, like buy a house, and he was looking out for my future.

Like I said, Jo and I went out just about every Friday and Saturday night to hear music. We could walk to so many of the little hole-in-the-wall nightclubs up on Haight. Besides Janis and Grace, there were the Beau Brummels, who I loved, a gifted young guitar player named Carlos Santana, and a group out of Walnut Creek called Country Joe and the Fish. In many ways, it reminded me of the old days in Eunice, when young musicians would bring their instruments and just play together for the love of it.

I also have to admit that I had a big crush on "Country" Joe MacDonald. He was just about the most handsome man I'd ever laid eyes on. Still, I knew he wasn't the one. That dark hair of his was the proof.

With Jo helping me pick out a new wardrobe, I felt like I fit in better on those nights out. My closet looked like it belonged to two different people, with one end still consisting of conservative work clothes and the other more free-wheeling and colorful stuff that I was coming to love.

I had Jo take some pictures of me in my new duds and sent them to my sisters. Both Pauline and Julie said I looked like a hippy and wondered what I was thinking.

The truth was, I couldn't have been happier.

Jo insisted that I go with him to the Monterey Pop Festival. "I've already bought you a ticket, Raine. You have to come. Besides, you know half of the groups who will be there. It'll be like getting together with friends."

I hemmed and hawed, but of course I ultimately said yes.

I got Mr. Sterling to give me Friday off from work, and Jo and I left on Thursday night. My suitcase had some of the floaty peasant blouses Jo had helped me pick out, along with the jeans his friend Diane had painted with flowers.

I had never seen so many beautiful people in one place. The Monterey Fair Grounds was full of young people, dressed in colorful clothes, sharing food, drink and yes, if one were so inclined, drugs ... all waiting to hear the music over the next few days. I was glad that we had Jo's VW bus to sleep in; others were sleeping on the ground. I was never a good camper, even as a kid, so having shelter and actual mattresses would make a huge difference.

The weather was beautiful; just a little cool when the sun went down. We were comfortable with our shawls and wraps.

And the music! There were groups I knew, like the Jefferson Airplane, and Janis Joplin's band, from home. But there were people from all over on that stage: The Who, Otis Redding, Jimi Hendrix. They were all mind-blowing.

After the show on the first day, Jo and I went back to the camper and slept. The next morning, we were ready for more.

I danced and danced, with anyone and everyone around me. I flirted, I laughed ... I don't think I'd ever had a better time than I did that day. Joe MacDonald even came over and danced with me, and told me he thought I looked very pretty in my embroidered blouse and painted jeans.

That evening, I couldn't find Jo anywhere after the bands were finished playing. I checked the van, the showers, the port-a-lets. Nothing.

I was walking back to the van for the second time when Janis found me.

"Hey, Raine," she rasped, her south Texas accent thick. "Jo's at the first aid tent. I've been looking for you. He tried to get friendly with the wrong guy. C'mon."

She didn't have to tell me twice; I took off at a run across the grass, hoping I didn't slip and fall.

I ran into the tent calling Jo's name.

"He's kind of a mess," the doctor said. His back was to me, and he was bent over a cot. I could see that Jo's face was bloody and bruised.

"In fact, I don't know how much he'll be able to talk to you for a little while. Are you his ..."

"Neighbor. Friend. I'm his friend."

The doctor straightened and turned around. His golden curls were like a halo around one of the most beautiful faces I'd ever seen, and his blue eyes were kind.

"Doctor Nick Sterling," he said. "And you are?"

"Raine Broussard."

"I shouldn't laugh," he said around a warm chuckle, "but I have to ask: do you work in a San Francisco law office?"

"Mr. Sterling's nephew, I presume?"

He extended his hand. "The very same. I've heard a great deal about you from my uncle. Now, let me tell you what's happening with your friend. I've got him stabilized and I've called for an ambulance ..."

I admit that I wasn't paying the strictest attention, but I figured it was all written down. I couldn't stop thinking about my sister's prediction.

The bottom line was that Jo was going to need surgery; his eye socket had been broken when the fellow had beaten him up. The ambulance would take Jo to the hospital in downtown Monterey.

"I'll follow with the van," I said.

Jo gave me the key, trying to talk through his swollen mouth.

Doctor Sterling pressed a piece of paper into my hand. "This is my phone number, at home and at the Free Clinic where I work. Please, let me know how he is ... and let me take you to dinner after the festival is over."

❧ ❧

The doctors at Monterey General Hospital didn't waste any time. Jo was taken into emergency surgery and I paced the floor. When he was moved to a room, he almost looked worse than when they took him in, between new bruises and stitches.

I sat in the chair next to his hospital bed, reading the same magazine a dozen times before he spoke.

"Hey, Raine. That doctor fellow sure was cute. You should go out with him."

That was when I told my best friend about my sister's predictions.

"Well, maybe you're supposed to have two curly-haired blond soulmates," he said as I took his hand. "I'm glad you're my friend."

"Me too, Jo. Me too."

I called Mr. Sterling to tell him about my friend's medical emergency ... and that I'd met his nephew. "I need to stay here with Jo until he can check out," I explained. "I'll make up the time at weekends if I have to."

"I can get a Kelly girl in here for a couple of days, Miss Broussard. You're a good friend, and a good person. I'm glad you and Nick finally got to meet, even if I don't like the circumstances. Please, don't worry. Your job is safe."

I really am a pretty lucky person.

I called the neighbor who was feeding Pearl, to let her know what had happened and that we'd be a little longer getting home. She was horrified, of course, and hoped that Jo would be all right. Then I called the salon. Luckily, Jo was popular with his colleagues and clients, and they were more than willing to hold his chair for him.

❦

The nurses let me use a shower in the hospital and I was able to change my clothes. I bought a book to read, and I stayed with Jo until the nurses made me leave each night. I slept in the van.

I finally called Nick Sterling the day that Jo was released, saying that we were on our way back to San Francisco and thanking him for all that he'd done.

"The best thanks you can give me is to have dinner with me. There's a funky old place called Sam Wo's in Chinatown. Do you know it? Meet me there tonight."

I agreed, and Jo and I got on the road.

Once I had Jo ensconced in his apartment, pain medication on board and Pearl purring in his lap, I went to my own apartment and collapsed. I set an alarm so that I'd be up in time for my dinner date.

৵৵ ৶৶

I chose one of my favorite gauzy peasant blouses and another pair of painted jeans Jo had brought me from Diane's Melrose boutique. I made sure my makeup was okay and hopped on the Muni bus to Chinatown rather than deal with parking my car.

Standing right outside the door to Sam Wo, wearing a brown turtleneck sweater and brown and green striped pants, was the man I was sure my sister Pauline meant for me. Nick kissed me hello and we went in to dinner.

He held the door open for me. "I feel like this is the beginning of something big."

I couldn't have agreed more.

Dark Days in Memphis

April 4, 1968

Raine was still shaking when she and Nick got off the plane in Baton Rouge. She hoped against hope that what she'd overheard in San Francisco was wrong.

It had to be wrong. He was a minister. Surely things like that didn't happen to men of God.

He was someone Raine knew, for goodness' sake. She'd walked with him, and so many others, back in 1963. She'd gone up to Washington with a girlfriend, who'd basically stolen her brother's car.

"We need to be part of history, Lorraine. We need to be there."

And so they were, listening to folk musicians ... and to one of the most amazing speeches Raine had ever heard.

I can't even remember that girl's name.

The two young women went back to Cajun country forever changed. Both of them learned by harsh experience not to talk about where they'd been; the redneck boys who called them "n— lovers" for believing in equality would never understand. For as low as Cajuns were on the social ladder, blacks would always be lower. Some folks took that as a strange point of pride.

Raine was not one of them.

Pauline and Julie thought her youthful idealism was a phase that their baby sister Lorraine would outgrow. That she would settle down with some fellow she met at a fais-do-do or church social, have a bunch of babies, and forget all of that social justice nonsense.

Instead, she'd gone to secretarial school in Baton Rouge and moved off to California, of all the damn things. At least she'd got herself engaged to a doctor. And if his curly blonde hair was a little longer than the local folks might have liked, well, everyone knew that he made a good living out there in San Francisco and that Raine, as she wanted to be called now, was able to quit her job when Nick Stirling moved into her Cole Street apartment in preparation for the wedding.

That was why they were back in Louisiana seven months after they met: to get married in front of her friends and family.

When Pauline, with little Harmon in tow and her belly big with another baby, stood up to meet them, all Raine could do was ask whether it was true, what she'd heard. Had that good, honorable man been murdered at the Memphis hotel that bore her name?

Pauline tried to draw her attention to the weather, the wedding ... anything else. Raine would not be moved. She walked over to the news stand and bought a copy of the New Orleans Times-Picayune, the front page of which confirmed her fears.

"Martin is dead," she sobbed, as Nick held her in his arms.

It was a while before she calmed down enough to collect their suitcases.

Christmas on Cole Street

December 3, 1968

"Raine Sterling, if you do not sit down and let me play host, I will send you and Nick back downstairs." Jo Cooper was completely recovered from the unfortunate incidents of the previous summer, and downright manic. "And that means no watching that handsome Presley boy on my new color television, so I'd be careful if I were you."

Nick laughed. "You'd better do as he says; there's too much moo goo gai pan here for him to eat by himself, and those delivery boys aren't cheap."

Raine sat down next to her husband on the cushion-covered sofa. She was grateful to Nick for many things, not the least of which was his understanding and friendship with her flamboyant buddy.

"I know when I'm outnumbered."

Nick reached over and ruffled her hair; she was letting it grow out, and the pixie of last summer was now a long fall of dark brown just past her shoulders. Jo trimmed her bangs that evening, covering her gauzy blouse with a towel. He'd refused to let shears touch his own locks, and his curls lay in golden ringlets down the middle of his back.

"You two are so beautiful." Jo said brought plates over to the coffee table. "The perfect hippie couple."

"Except one of us is a doctor," Raine laughed. "Shouldn't we be stone broke to be real hippies?"

"That's what they say. Oh, and dirty, too, if the rumors are to be believed. I guess you're not as perfect as I thought. Now, who wants egg foo yung?"

Jo served everyone and then turned serious.

"We need to talk about Christmas. I couldn't really celebrate last year because I was still kind of recuperating. And this means that neither of you know how much I love the holidays. I hope you will both come and have dinner with me on Christmas Eve ... turkey and all the trimmings. I'll make the main things and maybe you can bring something to share? I ask friends from work who don't have anyone, and believe me, in my line of work I know a lot of, well, other guys like me whose families won't have them anymore. So, everyone brings a dish to share, draws names to exchange gifts, sing songs ... the whole thing. Please say you'll come. Please."

Nick and Raine exchanged looks.

"Well, Jo, we'd planned to ask you to join us," Raine said. "But it looks as though you've turned the tables. I think it would be great fun to meet your friends, and to share the holiday with you. I hope you'll let me read a story to the group."

Raine told Jo and Nick about how her father would gather all the children, visitors and family alike, into the parlor.

"Everyone was in their pajamas, armed with a cup of cocoa, and snuggled up in blankets. Daddy would read 'T'was the Night Before Christmas' when we were little kids, and 'The Gift of the Magi' when we got older. Then we'd all go to bed. When we got up, Mommy had breakfast on the table, and there were presents from Santa Claus."

"I think that would be just grand," Jo said. "I suggest you stick with the poem this time; some of the fellows have a short attention span. Still, I'm delighted to add your tradition to the program."

He grabbed a nearby pad covered with scrawls and made another note.

"And yes, there really is a program. Otherwise, we'll forget to do half the things we set out to. Anyway, at the end of the evening we fix paper plates with leftovers and take them over to the soup kitchen. They're ready to hand out to hungry folks, and no one has to deal with a stuffed fridge full of things they'll never finish. We finish up by caroling there. I hope it doesn't sound too boring."

Nick opined that it sounded like a wonderful holiday and he was looking forward to it.

"I'm so glad." Jo replied. "Now, let's get the TV tuned in. I heard Elvis Presley wears a leather suit in this show, and I don't plan to miss it."

Help Wanted

Present Day

"I'm here about the job," Laurie said in her most resolute tone.

"I thought you might be, baby," Miss Julie replied. "Let's get you a seat. My nephew Amos will be back in just a minute; he's gone to pick up his daughter from school. Can I bring you something to drink?"

"Just a cup of coffee, black. Thank you"

Laurie Beaudry sat down where the elderly hostess told her to. Julie patted Laurie on the shoulder as she went for the coffee pot.

In that brief moment, she learned a great deal about the sad-eyed blond woman who presented herself at the Bayou Café.

So much like me, she thought. That no-account husband left her with a little boy and not near enough money. Trying to get a second job to make up the difference.

When Julie came back to the table, she had two cups of coffee and two slices of peach pie on a tray.

"Let's chat for a minute before Amos gets here," Julie said. "And not one word; the pie's my treat."

Peering at the woman across from her, Julie said "You were Laurie Parsons, weren't you? I remember you and your friends coming in here at lunch time when you all went to Ursulines."

"I'm surprised you remembered me, Miss Julie," Laurie replied. "You haven't changed a bit, and I've gotten so old. My son's in second grade at Bethune Elementary."

"Well, if that don't beat all! My great-niece goes to that school, too; she's in first grade and smart as a whip. We're all so proud of her."

As they chatted, Laurie relaxed a little. She hadn't wanted to let on that she'd been a customer so many years ago. Miss Julie was ageless even then, and she'd always seemed to know who needed comforting and who needed teasing. That was clearly still the case.

Miss Julie put down her coffee cup.

"Are you sure you want a second job, when you work so hard over there on Royal Street by night? And in such a fancy place compared to us?"

Laurie felt like crying.

"You always seemed to see right through us," she rejoined.

"You didn't answer my question," Julie said, gently.

"It's not a matter of want, it's a case of need. I need to see to my boy, Johnny. I need to have money to afford a good place, and a babysitter, and for him to have some extras."

"That surely is admirable," Julie said.

"And I don't want to leave our apartment ... at least, not while Johnny's in school here. He's too little to take the bus by himself. I want him to be okay."

The bell over the café door rang as Amos, Diana, and Evie entered the building.

"Tante Julie," Amos greeted her with a kiss on her papery cheek. "Now my three favorite girls are here."

"You are a wicked flirt, Amos Boudreaux. I'm going to tell your pretty wife on you."

Diana and Evie came over to hug Julie.

"He's terrible, isn't he?" Diana laughed. "I'm glad he's mine."

"Ms. Beaudry!" Evie said. "What are you doing here? Daddy, her son is two years ahead of me at Bethune. He's real nice, talks to me on the playground and whatnot."

Laurie stood up and extended her hand. "Mister Boudreaux, I'm here about the job."

As Amos shook Laurie's hand, he saw Julie give a nearly imperceptible nod.

"Well, we're not too fancy here," he said. "You can call me Amos. Let me show you around the back of the house and we'll talk."

As they disappeared toward the kitchen, Julie took the "Help Wanted" sign out of the window.

Damaged

Present Day

"I'm terribly sorry, sir," Laurie responded to the irate customer. "I'll bring you another plate."

"I'm a busy man," he replied, his face turning red under a flawless blond businessman's haircut. Soon his face would match the color of his power tie. "I expect a replacement breakfast, on the double."

Laurie flinched as she collected the offending plate and hurried back to the pass-through.

"Felix, this was supposed to be over-easy, not sunny-side up. He wants a new plate."

"He ate more than half of it," the cook observed.

"I know."

Laurie leaned her hip against the counter and wiped away the tears that threatened to spill over. She'd worked a banquet the previous night at Brennan's, which kept her up later than usual. Still, she was right on time for her morning shift at the Bayou Café.

The angry customer buttonholed Miss Julie, who was coming around with the coffee pot. He was gesturing frantically toward the kitchen.

Felix passed a new plate to Laurie and she hurried out just in time to hear the man announce that his breakfast should be on the house because it was taking so long.

Miss Julie laid a comforting hand on his shoulder. Then she spoke.

"You ate well over half of that food before you sent Miss Laurie here back to the kitchen. Now, don't you interrupt me. I know it's true, and so do you. She's here with a new plate. Now, you take it and you pay your check like a gentleman."

Laurie sat the plate down on the table, along with the check folder.

"Since you're in a hurry and all," she said.

"I'll have both of your jobs for this," the man sputtered.

"Would you like to make a formal complaint to the owner?" Miss Julie's lips turned up in a wry smile.

"Why, now that you mention it, I would," he huffed.

"Miss Laurie, would you go get Amos from the back? I'll finish pouring coffee for the rest of the folks and meet you back at this fine man's table."

Laurie turned without a word and went to Amos' office in the back of the building. Her eyes downcast, she told him what had happened ... and waited.

Amos stood up slowly; it was apparent that he was trying hard to control his temper. He took off his plaid flannel over-shirt, revealing-muscular arms straining the sleeves of his Tulane University t-shirt. He ran his finger through his black hair and swore in Cajun French.

"All right, Miss Laurie. Let's go see this couillon."

Despite having a school-age child, Amos Boudreaux remained an imposing physical specimen. His broad shoulders and slim hips still turned heads when he passed on the street; his muscular physique could have belonged to a much younger man.

"You wanted to see me, sir?"

The businessman gulped. "You're the owner?"

"Yes, sir, I am. Now, I'd like to hear your side of the story Miss Laurie here just told me." He leaned over the table, resting his weight on one hand ... which put an imposing bicep right at the angry man's eye level.

"It was just a misunderstanding about my eggs, sir. Everything is fine now."

"I'm so glad to hear it," Amos replied softly. "I would hate to think someone was giving one of my valued staff members trouble when there was no cause for complaint."

"No harm done," the man replied, flinching under Amos' steely, dark gaze.

"Are you sure?"

"Yes, sir, I am."

"Good. Now, why don't you finish your breakfast? I'll look after you for the rest of your meal."

Julie and Laurie exchanged a look and went back to the prep area together. The rest of the breakfast crowd was thinning out and they tallied the morning's checks.

Amos came back with the angry man's check folder and handed it to Laurie.

"I think you'll find he was generous with his tip." A smile played on Amos' thin lips. "When you're done here, Laurie, please see me in my office." He strode through the kitchen doors without a backward glance.

"Well, there goes my job," Laurie said."

"Girl, that boy ain't mad with you," Julie replied. "I promise. Now, go see him."

When Laurie went into the office, Amos was sitting at his desk, his head in his hands. He looked up when Laurie came in and indicated a nearby chair.

"Have a seat, Laurie."

"I am so sorry ..."

"No," he interrupted. "Don't apologize."

"But ..."

"No." Amos sighed. "Your job is in no danger. You did nothing wrong, okay? Now, I'm going to ask you something that might be none of my business. And don't you feel shy about telling me so. But something about this situation made me wonder. Your husband. Did he abuse you?"

"How did you know?"

"Because I saw how your posture changed and how you rushed to take the blame for someone else's behavior."

"He ... Anthony ... always talked kind of mean to me. He hit me a few times before he left. Johnny saw it happen."

"Are you getting help?"

"Help? Mister Boudreaux, I'm working two jobs to make ends meet. I don't have time to get help. I don't even have time to get a divorce lawyer."

Laurie started to cry. Amos handed her a tissue and she dried her eyes.

"I'm sorry ..."

"Don't apologize. And for the love of God, call me Amos." He smiled. "I can find you someone to talk to. And I'm a lawyer, god damn it. Let me help."

"I don't know. It doesn't feel right."

"Why not?"

"I ... well, what will your wife think, you doing this for me?"

"Let's ask her."

Amos called Diana and she said she was on her way. Sure enough, before long the plump little brunette came through the door, leaning on her cane. Amos greeted her with a kiss and gave her his arm to lean on. Laurie didn't think she'd ever seen a man look at a woman with more love in his eyes than the way Amos looked at Diana.

"Sweetheart, you know Laurie Beaudry. I'm going to help her draw up divorce papers, so she can be free of a man who abused her."

Diana sat down next to Laurie.

"I'm so glad, Amos."

"You are?" Laurie was incredulous.

"Yes. No one should be tied to someone who is cruel. We wind up feeling as though we are the damaged ones. We start to feel worthless because we let someone else define who we are. I know first-hand what that's like; I had someone leave me when I got sick. I felt so bad that I was afraid to tell Amos that I was living with a disease. I knew I was falling in love, and I didn't want him to leave."

Diana leaned over to touch Laurie's arm.

"You're not damaged, Laurie. But you need to be free. Not just for you, but for your boy. Let Amos and me help you take those first steps."

Laurie could only nod through her tears.

Laurie got to the café late one day; her car wouldn't start, and she took the bus across town. She started to apologize to Miss Julie, who merely waved her off.

"Girl, sometimes those things happen. Now, take a minute to calm yourself and listen to the music; I've got the tables covered."

Indeed, there was music. Amos was sitting with another man; both of them were playing guitar. The second man had dark hair and blue eyes; there was a distinct family resemblance between the two. He was singing an old Dorsey Burnette song about how he fell in love in Texas, and the two ... brothers, Laurie supposed ... were grinning from ear to ear and clearly enjoying themselves. After the song was over, Laurie joined the customer and staff in their applause.

And then a penny dropped for her.

As Amos was putting away his guitar, she approached him.

"I'll get to work in just a second, I promise. But I need to ask you something. You were the singer for Big Muddy back in the day, weren't you?"

"Guilty as charged," he smiled. "That was a long time ago."

"I loved your band. I'm sure I still have a tape somewhere."

"Amos," the other man interrupted, "are you going to introduce me to this lovely lady?"

"Laurie, this is my brother Riley. Well-known gad-about and rolling stone, trifling man, and fatal charmer. Watch yourself."

Riley winked at Laurie. "He always says the nicest things about me."

⁂

No one was terribly surprised when Riley asked Laurie out. Pretty soon the two were keeping regular company, and Riley invited Laurie out to one of the family gatherings. The two were sitting off to one side of the deck, watching as one of the young boys showed Johnny around .. with great emphasis on making sure his Uncle Amos was introduced properly.

"You see how Jimmy idolizes Amos?" Riley said. "Well, that's the way I was with my uncle Nick. He met my Aunt Raine ... Lorraine is her name ... at the Monterey Pop Festival. He was the doctor there. Raine's friend Jo made a pass at the wrong guy and got himself beaten up. Nick patched Jo up enough to get him into the ambulance. Anyway, he and Raine fell in love and got married out in San Francisco, and they came to visit from time to time. I thought Nick was the most amazing guy I'd ever seen, with this long curly hair in a ponytail and wearing hippie clothes. He knew how to make anything that hurt stop with a kind word and a band-aid, and that's what I thought doctoring was about. Working in the free clinic and helping people in need. My version of that was going to medical school and joining Doctors Without Borders.

"Well, Nick retired a few years into the AIDS epidemic. Raine was holding Jo's hand when he died in hospice, and he realized he just couldn't do it anymore. They'd put money aside for years, so they gave up their apartment in San Francisco and bought a little house in this town called Port Costa. It's kind of a wide spot in the road north of Berkeley. There are two restaurants, one of 'em fancy and the other one a dive bar in what used to be a grain warehouse. The mayor is this wild, silver-haired rockabilly singer who puts me in mind of Harmon. Oh, and City Hall is in the same building as the dive bar. The hotel used to be the whorehouse when the town was a real port. It's just this sleepy little place now.

"After some of the stuff I saw in Syria, Nick and Raine suggested I come to visit them. So, I got in the boat and went. Nick knew that the only thing that would help was time, see, because he'd been through it. Vietnam veterans, homeless people, AIDS patients ... he'd seen it all, and still said it was nothing compared to trying to get tear gas out of little kids' eyes, or comforting a mom holding a dead baby. I needed the peace to get my shit together. And it worked."

Disappearing Act

Present Day

Laurie parked the rental car in the lot at the end of Port Costa's only street. She wasn't sure what she planned to accomplish. Miss Julie had given her Nick and Raine's address, and she knew she was just around the corner from finding out where he'd gone – both literally and figuratively. She helped Johnny out of the booster seat in the back and took his hand as she looked around.

There was the dive bar on her left as she looked up the road. She'd passed the town's solitary school and church on her way in. She saw the hotel sign and smiled to herself as she recalled what Riley had said about it.

"Hold my hand," she said to Johnny, who obliged. "These sidewalks are a little rough and I don't want you to get hurt."

"What is this place, Mommy?"

"Well, we're going to see Mister Riley's aunt and uncle," she said as they walked up the street. "He said he came to visit them when times got rough, and I'm hoping they'll know where he is."

She checked the house numbers and found the one she was looking for. An orange cat sat on the porch and meowed a greeting. Johnny let go of Laurie's hand to pet the animal as his mother rang the bell.

Despite her hopes, Laurie was still surprised when Riley answered the door. The entire speech she'd planned to deliver to Nick or Raine went out of her head as she looked into his blue eyes.

"Mister Riley!" Johnny exclaimed when he saw him. "We were coming to see your auntie and uncle. Are you visiting them too?"

"I sure am, squirt," Riley replied. "Come on in."

Laurie and Johnny followed him into the little living room.

"Nick and Raine went up to Sacramento for the day," he said. "There's a big flea market up there once a month that they like. Can I get you something to drink?"

"Mister Riley, don't you like Mommy and me anymore?" Johnny asked before Laurie could answer Riley's question.

"John Michael Beaudry!" Laurie was mortified. Even though she'd come looking for Riley, she wasn't ready to be that direct.

Riley sat down on the couch and gestured for Johnny to sit next to him. "It's okay, squirt. The truth is, I got scared. It happens to grown-ups, too. So, I came to the one place where I know I can always get over being scared."

"You ran away because you were scared?"

"That's about the size of it."

"When I'm scared, Mommy makes sure I have my teddy bear and gives me a hug. Is that what your aunt and uncle do to help you?"

"In a way, it is. But here's the most important thing. I shouldn't have been scared; I should have been excited. Like the way you get with fireworks, or a Ferris wheel at the fair, you know? Because what scared me is how much I love you and your mommy ... and I didn't know if she'd have me."

He looked up at Laurie, who had been standing across the room from him and just watching the exchange.

"Oh, god, Riley. I have never loved anyone the way I love you. I came all this way to find you, just as afraid of you telling me to go back to New Orleans as I could possibly be."

"I do want you go to back, Laurie," he said as he stood up and took her into his arms. "But I want to be there with you."

Flowers of Europe

Flowers of London

1882 Thaddeus Flowers awoke in a bed not his own, head pounding. He'd definitely taken too much ale at the White Horse last night, and was not entirely sure where he was. The pub was in the Seven Dials, but he might be anywhere from there to Chelsea.

Raking his fingers through his dark hair, Thad sat up slowly. The dull light filtering in through the curtains showed a respectable enough room; his clothes were draped across a chair ... on top of what looked like a petticoat.

Oh, dear god.

Thad looked at the sleeping figure next to him. The young woman's auburn hair was spread across the pillow, her face serene in sleep.

A pretty girl. I wish I remembered her name!

With movements that were far too practiced even for his own liking, Thad slid out of bed without disturbing the redhead. All clothes except for his boots were donned quietly. Once outside the room, and the house, he would put on his boots and walk away.

As he'd done so many times before.

Of course, that had been in America. Thad had promised himself that he'd be better behaved once he moved to London. But the women all seemed to adore his handsome face and charming accent ... and so, here he was again.

Tiptoeing out of what seemed to be a respectable boarding house, Thad paused to slip on his boots and get his bearings. There was Covent Garden, and Drury Lane. So, not far from Seven Dials at all.

Very well, then.

Thad hailed a cab to take him back to his own boarding house in Baker Street. During the ride, he reflected on how he came to London in the first place.

Thaddeus Bartholomew Flowers was born in Placerville, California, on July 4, 1861. His father, William, had struck gold on his claim after many years' effort and, upon doing so, promptly married a young woman with aspirations toward social climbing. While William was plain, with a long face and thinning brown hair, his bride was a lively blonde girl with a quick laugh, sparkling eyes, and a lush figure. She had caught his attention some while back, and when he asked the girl's father for permission to call, it was given quickly. William was 26; his bride was ten years younger.

Martha Jane Flowers' insistence upon giving Thad what William called a "high-falutin' name" was born of those aspirations. She was determined that her son would not grow up in what the locals called Hangtown, a rough frontier sort of place with a single main street comprised mainly of saloons. The local constabulary was aided by the kind of rough justice that saw vigilantes throwing rope nooses over tree limbs and taking matters into their own hands. This was not, Martha Jane proclaimed regularly, the kind of environment in which one might raise a gentleman. So, the family moved to San Francisco.

It must be said that Martha Jane's concept of what constituted a gentleman came directly from the pages of her favorite romance novels; she had a subscription to Placerville's tiny lending library, and devoured books like Pride & Prejudice, Five Weeks in a Balloon, or Miss Marjoribanks almost as soon as they were available.

Thaddeus was not inclined toward school; he was more of a dreamer. He wanted to have adventures of the sort he read about in the dime novels. He greatly admired the soldiers he saw strolling in and out of the Presidio of San Francisco in their uniforms, and entertained the idea that the army might be a ticket to such adventure one day. He didn't seem to notice the suffering veterans of the War Between the States, only six years past. His child's mind thought only of the glamour of seeing new places.

This was Martha Jane's greatest legacy to her son: an ambition to see bigger and better things, and to leave the whole idea of small towns behind.

During Thad's eleventh year, William and Martha Jane welcomed a baby daughter to the household. Lavinia Clementine Flowers was the apple of her parents' eye, and Thad alternated between feeling like a proud older brother and as though he were invisible. So much focus was on the new baby, who was somewhat unexpected. Thad was old enough to understand that Martha Jane thought she could not have another child. The little girl's blond curls and blue eyes seemed to enchant everyone who saw her.

Then the measles came to San Francisco. Miraculously enough, neither of the children caught the disease. Martha Jane, who had gone to help nurse a neighbor's child, came down with it. She stayed with that neighbor in order to avoid exposing her own children.

She never came home.

After Martha Jane's death, William Flowers didn't spend much time mourning. With two children at home, one of them a baby who still needed the bottle, he needed to find a wife. There was one young woman who decided that William's wealth was more than adequate inducement to put up with what she privately called "an ugly face attached to a couple of brats"; Melanie Carson Dennis was entering her second season and about to turn twenty. With her glossy black hair, willowy figure, and brilliant green eyes, she could not have been more different from the late Martha Jane in appearance if she tried. She also differed from Martha Jane in that she never cared for books; they required too much effort.

Thaddeus hated her.

❧ ❧

On his eighteenth birthday, Thaddeus left home. William gave him an advance on his inheritance and wished him well. Thad chose London as his destination, working his way across country on the railroads until he could get passage on a ship. During his time on the rails, he became interested in mechanics, and got an idea for an airship. In his spare moments, he created drawing after drawing of the device.

Thad's sketches showed a ten-person gondola, painted white and trimmed with gold around the top and on the rudder. The gondola was painted with beautiful creatures from mythology, like Pegasus and Unicorn, and hung from three large balloons in shades of pink and blue to match the other decorations. The idea behind the airship was to lighten the traffic of London streets; it didn't have to go very high, Thad reasoned, just above the buildings. Notes on the side of his first drawing indicated that lap rugs and warm drinks would be provided to passengers, and that eventually a fleet of the ships would parallel the routes of the horse-drawn omnibuses that covered the city.

Thad kept up a correspondence with his younger sister; Vinie was the only one he wrote to anymore. Vinie confided that she kept his letters secret, her ten-year-old's enthusiasm making a game of the whole thing. She also told him that she thought his flying machine idea was "just grand," and that she hoped one day to see it in action.

§

As the cab passed the Tower of London, Thad envisioned his beautiful airship sailing overhead to dock there. Perhaps even Her Royal Majesty would ride in the painted gondola, traveling through the sky instead of stuck in a carriage! She could take the airship from Buckingham to the Tower and be there in a trice!

Right now, Thad needed to worry about the present instead of either the past or the future.

His landlady, Mrs. Hudson, had introduced him to a fellow boarder. That peculiar chap was interested in all manner of science, so Thad showed him the sketches he'd made. Young Mr. Holmes had drawn a circle around the three balloons and written "This won't be practical; how will you heat them equally?" in a tidy hand. That led to a lengthy discussion about engineering the airship, as well as what fare to charge ("How will you beat a half-penny seat on the omnibus," Holmes asked). There was so much more to it than Thad had first thought.

In the end, Holmes recommended that Thad visit the Crystal Palace to see the electricity exhibition. That might be just what he needed to get his concept off the ground, both literally and figuratively. And that was the plan for today.

But first, Thad needed to take care of his hangover.

He paid the cab driver and went into the boarding house, hoping against hope that Mrs. Hudson would still be abed.

His prayers were dashed when the formidable lady met him in the hallway.

"Breakfast is waiting for you on the sideboard, Mister Flowers. I was rather concerned when you did not come home last night; your supper went to waste."

"My apologies, Mrs. Hudson. The time got away from me, you see, and I stayed with a friend."

"A friend. Is that what you call those women, Mr. Flowers?" Thad wasn't sure, but he thought he saw a hint of a smile on the woman's face. "In any event, sir, please do break your fast. And let me know if you'll be, er, staying with a friend again this evening so that I may plan accordingly."

Thad dared a little smile of his own. "Yes, ma'am."

After bolting his breakfast, Thad went up to his rather messy room to change clothes and shave. He hoped to talk with someone like Thomas Edison or Nikola Tesla at the exhibition; surely one of those greats would give him the information he needed to set his idea in motion. He grabbed his plans from a precariously tall stack of books, put them into a portfolio, and ran out to hail yet another cab for Hyde Park.

❧ ☙

Inside the Crystal Palace, there were more exhibits than he could ever have imagined: nine different kinds of lightbulbs, just for a start.

To his chagrin, neither Edison nor Tesla were present; they were represented solely by their inventions and an assistant here and there showing off various devices.

An exhibit showing an electric motor caught Thad's attention, and he looked around for the man who had invented it. Surely that would be the answer to at least part of his problem. There was no scientist to be seen ... but there was a young woman, dark-haired and wasp-waisted in a fashionable gown of celadon green and wine brocade. Perhaps she was the inventor's daughter. Thad put his most charming smile on his face, and addressed her.

"Excuse me, miss? Hello, I'm Thaddeus Flowers. I would like to speak to the man who invented this engine."

She turned to face Thad, and he was struck silent by her beauty. She had the most amazing eyes he'd ever seen; they sparkled like emeralds in a high-street jeweler's window.

"I'm Arabella Abingdon, And I am the 'man' who invented this engine."

It took Thad a moment to recover from his surprise. Trying to behave as though a female scientist were the most natural thing in the world, he took out his design to show her.

She examined the drawings and made notations along the side with a pencil she pulled from behind her ear: equations that That couldn't even begin to follow. After a moment, she stopped and spoke.

"Your idea is an interesting one, Mister Flowers. I would like to discuss it with you further. Perhaps over dinner?"

It was as bold a proposition as any man might have made. After a second's hesitation, Thad accepted.

"There is a public house nearby, the Three Tuns," Arabella continued. "I will meet you there at six o'clock this evening. And now, I must return to my work. I can hardly sell my engine design if I don't publicize it, you know."

She extended her hand, and Thad bowed over it. Afterwards, she turned her back to him, and gave her attention to another man who was examining the engine with great curiosity.

Thad would be counting the hours until six o'clock.

❧ ❧

When Thaddeus Flowers awoke the next morning, he was in his own rooms on Baker street .. with no recollection of how he got there.

The drawings of his airship were gone.

She couldn't have. Surely not. Could she?

Flowers of Paris

1889

Thaddeus Flowers awoke in a bed not his own, head pounding. He'd definitely taken too much absinthe at the Café des Artistes last night, and was not entirely sure where he was. The bistro was in Montmartre, but he could be anywhere from there to St. Michel.

Raking his fingers through his dark hair, Thad sat up slowly. The dull light filtering in through the curtains showed a respectable enough room; his clothes were draped across a chair ... on top of what looked like a petticoat.

Oh, dear god. Not again.

This really was becoming a habit ... and one that Thad needed to break.

Eventually.

The girl sat up and pushed her blonde hair out of her eyes. "You can leave the money on the washstand as always, Thad."

Thank God, it was only Colette. Thad was a regular in her crib.

"Who is Arabella," Colette asked as Thad dumped a handful of coins next to the bowl and pitcher. At his surprised look, she explained. "You talk in your sleep."

Thad shrugged his shoulders, dressed himself, and stepped into the harsh morning light. He squinted as he made his way to the shady side of the street and walked to his own garret room. The concierge, Madame Solange, would probably not be up yet – he hoped. He was in no mood for her lectures, and he needed to sober up for his meeting that afternoon in the Marais.

Arabella Abingdon. He could hardly wait to see her again. It had been what, seven years since they'd met in London? He'd never forgotten her striking beauty, her intellect – who knew that a woman could understand science so clearly? And now, she had someone in Paris who could help him make his dream of airship transportation in cities come true.

Or so she said.

Back in his room, Thad re-read the letter for what seemed like the hundredth time:

"My dear Thaddeus:

You must meet me Thursday next, four o'clock in the afternoon, at the address below. A long-ago friend from my boarding school days has married an absolute genius. I showed him your plans, and he's made a model for your flying machine. Don't be late.

A.A."

The address was a townhouse in the Place des Vosges; Thaddeus had made a preliminary trip to look at the place. A fashionable address, to be sure; probably the home of an old man in his dotage who had taken a young wife. Still, curiosity compelled him to be there at the appointed time. Especially since he'd never managed to adequately recreate his flying machine concept; other drafts just felt wrong after Arabella's disappearance, and after a while he abandoned the entire project.

Now it was that Thursday. Thad laid out his clothes, brushed the dust from the fashionable frock coat, and made sure he had clean linen. He would wait to shave until closer to departure time; that way, he would present a better impression. A look in the glass suggested a trip to his barber might be in order, but the funds he'd paid Colette were the last in his pocket. That also meant a trip to the bank.

So much for the quiet day he'd planned to pass before the appointment.

◈ ◈

Arabella Abingdon had been the stuff of dreams, for the most part. Their dinner together ended in her rooms off Manchester Square. There, Thaddeus had yet another surprise; he had never imagined that a woman could match his ardor in bed – unless, of course, she was a prostitute, in which case, one never could be truly sure. As it had not occurred to him that a woman could be his intellectual equal, so it had never crossed his mind that a woman might have physical desires of her own.

The entire experience was eye-opening for him. Then, as quickly as they'd met, she was gone – to Menlo Park, New Jersey … if the address on her first letter to him was anything to go by. Letters after that came from all over the world.

And now, both of them were in Paris.

☙ ❧

Thaddeus presented his card to the majordomo who answered the door. He was a trifle disturbed to note that the servant was better dressed than himself. He wondered who his tailor might be, and whether it was an appropriate question to ask of the proverbial help. The man was tall and slim, with dark blond hair and a fashionable Van Dyke beard; he leaned heavily on a cane when he walked but still retained an air of dignity. Thad followed the fellow down a hallway that opened onto a parlor. There, he found Arabella sitting with a chestnut-haired beauty.

"Thank you, Gilbert." The latter stood to greet their guest. "I'm Claire LeMaître. You must be Monsieur Flowers. Arabella has spoken highly of you." She extended her hand.

Thad took her hand and bowed over it, a trifle surprised to be greeted in English. "I am delighted to meet you, Madame LeMaître. Miss Abingdon tells me you were at school together."

"Yes, we were at the same boarding school in Switzerland. Before we go to meet my husband, would you like some tea?"

Thad declined, so Claire asked Gilbert to let the maestro know that they would be joining him in his study shortly.

"I should warn you, Monsieur Flowers, that my husband suffers a physical deformity that embarrasses him greatly. He will be masked; do not let it frighten you."

Thaddeus nodded his understanding, trying to contain his excitement at seeing his design in action. He and Arabella followed Claire down the hall.

"Where did you get my drawings," he whispered. "I've wanted to ask you that for ages."

"You gave them to me, Thad."

"I did?"

"Yes, you did. I should have known you wouldn't recall; you'd had rather too much whiskey when you asked for my help. And there was no reason you couldn't have asked, other than your own embarrassment, given all of the letters we've exchanged." Arabella seemed poised to say a great deal more on the matter, but their conversation was cut short by Claire opening the door to her husband's study and ushering them in.

✈ ✈

Monsieur LeMaître was not, as Thaddeus had expected, an elderly man. In fact, he was not yet middle-aged, tall and well-built. The unmasked side of his face was that of the most elegant dandy; his black hair was perfectly cut and his green-gold eyes riveting. The hand he extended to Thaddeus was long and elegant, the handshake demonstrated a grip of steel.

The masked man kissed his wife on the cheek, and held chairs so that she and Arabella could be seated.

"Monsieur Flowers, I have wanted to meet you ever since Mademoiselle Abingdon showed me your sketches. I will show you the model I made, which improves on your design."

"Please, call me Thaddeus or Thad. Monsieur Flowers makes me think you want to talk to my father."

"Then you must call me Erik. Now, to the business at hand."

He led Thaddeus to a table near the window, where a copy of his sketch was held down by weights at each corner. In addition to Arabella's equations, there were additional sketches, more equations in a different hand that could only be Erik's, and the entire balloon segment lined through.

"You see, I looked at what you had originally planned with the balloon. It is impractical either with your original three balloons or a larger single one as with the new idea you concocted with Mademoiselle Abingdon. You looked at her engine as a way to create steam to make the balloon rise, but you failed to take into account the condensation that would inevitably develop inside the bag itself, rendering the balloon useless. No, my young monsieur, you only thought it partway through."

"I beg to differ, sir. I spent years working on this concept."

"Then I am surprised that you failed to consider the easiest way to make your airship work. Remember, there is no need to overcomplicate things. You need not rig something complicated, for example, to make a backdrop fall to the stage; you have only to untie the ropes that hold it in place."

What a peculiar example. What on earth would make a man create such an analogy?

"In any event, I did some more calculations, and then revisited the works of Leonardo da Vinci to confirm my thoughts. Thus, I have created a scale model of your airship ... using Mademoiselle Abingdon's engine and my improvements."

He opened a drawer and took out what looked like a small boat. It was Thaddeus' beautifully painted gondola in miniature, complete with ten little dolls as passengers, all fashionably attired. Their clothing was to scale, right down to the hats. Each had a lap rug over his or her knees. Unlike Thad's design with the three balloons, there were a series of blades at different places on the exterior, the same gold as the boat's trim. Another departure from Thad's design was the domed glass covering on the boat, which would render the gondola weatherproof. The metal framework holding the glass in place was a series of elegant curlicues that hid the joints.

"That's very pretty." Thaddeus was a trifle disappointed.

"It's more than pretty." Erik's tone was dry. He flicked a switch on the back of what Thaddeus could only think of as a toy and a tiny motor could be heard warming up. Soon the blades began to spin, faster and faster. The little gondola scooted across the table and into Erik's elegant hand. He held it aloft ... and let it go.

Thaddeus was sure that it was going to crash to the ground ... but it didn't. Instead, it flew straight until Erik retrieved it to stop it from hitting the wall.

"Of course, you'd have someone operating the tiller to steer." Erik pointed to an elevated seat in the back with a uniformed doll before he switched off the motor. "My friend, your basic idea is pure genius. It will revolutionize travel in large cities. You just need to have competent boatbuilders, ironworkers, and glaziers to make it for you. Now, if you'll excuse me, I have an opera to compose." The masked man bowed gravely and exited, closing the door behind himself.

"An opera? Really? I thought you said this man was an inventor."

"He's more than that, Thad," Arabella replied. "If you ever want a full character of Maestro Erik LeMaître, you could ask around the Opéra Garnier. They will tell you stories that will make you think you're in the midst of a penny dreadful. But that's really not the point, is it?

I think I understand the backdrop story now.

Arabella turned to hug her friend. "Thank you again, Claire, for arranging this meeting. I have every confidence that Mister Flowers here will be in touch regarding the necessary schematics. I will call on you again tomorrow. Thad, let us be gone."

Gilbert, the majordomo, held the outer door open after Thad and Arabella had donned hats and wraps.

Arabella tucked her gloved hand into the crook of Thad's elbow. "I think, my friend, that you and I need to go celebrate."

Erik came to the door as they were leaving. "Monsieur Flowers, if I could have one more word with you, please."

Thaddeus followed him down the hallway, Arabella and Gilbert waiting in puzzlement.

"I would suggest, if you intend to woo Mademoiselle Abingdon, that you spend a little less time in bistros and a little more at her side. Open your hand, sir." Thaddeus did so, and Erik dropped two metal disks into his palm. "Take her to see that godawful tower of Eiffel's that they've just opened at the Universal Exposition, and then take her to the opera tonight. You can return the tokens later. Good day to you, sir."

Thaddeus thanked him, and put the tokens in his inside coat pocket, after noting where he and Arabella would be seated for that evening's performance at the Opéra Garnier.

Box Five.

It Happened in Memphis

miss in that old-fashioned attire. The affection among the group was apparent, and I couldn't help wondering whether the actors were a real-life family.

I turned to ask my dad what he thought of the little reenactment I was watching, but he was focused on helping Mom get under the tiny awning. After making sure she was settled, he pulled a handkerchief out of his pocket and swiped at his face and hair, focused solely on drying off a little before we went inside.

"Mom, did you notice the reenactors over by the car? I think that's kind of neat."

"I'm sorry, Evie. I was concentrating on not slipping in the rain. Where did you see them again?"

When I turned to show her, the people and their things were gone. The car was alone on display ... and completely empty.

"I guess they went inside to get out of the rain," I said.

"We should do the same," Mom replied.

We went into the dark brown building and my dad paid for our tickets. We would see a little museum, a church presentation (of all things; I didn't think this was going to be a religious visit), and the tiny, two-room house in which Elvis Presley was born.

"Before we go into any of these places," he said, "I want to talk about why I think this trip is important. I know you love this music, Evie, but we need to remember that the legendary people whose records you listen to came from nothing. We're really fortunate with all we have, and sometimes it's worth a pause to remember. With that, let's look at this museum and then go over for the church program."

The Elvis mementos and memorabilia, all part of a private collection, were fascinating. No photos were allowed, but it was neat to see the clothes, books, and other things that had belonged to the man who really was the first rock star. I was still distracted by what I'd seen outside by the antique car that had belonged to Vernon and Gladys

Presley. The reenactors surely did look like the Presleys; their photos were in the museum and I studied them for a long time.

After a few minutes of wandering around the gift shop and picking out souvenirs, Dad gathered us together to walk over for the church program. The little one-room building had been the Presley's family church, the docent explained, as people in both modern-day and period clothing filed in. I sat down on one of the rear-most pews while the guide explained the multi-media presentation that would simulate a Pentecostal service for the visitors.

Just as both the screens and the lights were lowered, the blonde boy I saw earlier slipped in and sat beside me, his cap in his hand.

"Sure is somethin', ain't it?" he whispered. "Course, that fella up on the screen ain't quite as inspiring as Brother Frank Smith was when he got to going, but he does tolerably well."

"We shouldn't be talking," I whispered back.

Dad turned around and gave me a puzzled look.

"Nah, it's not really church. 'Sides, we used to really make a joyful noise during services." He gave a little lopsided smile that lit up his hooded blue eyes.

"You're really into this role; I admire you for it. I'm a performer myself."

The boy gave me that same smile. "I'm not a performer. Leastwise, not yet. I got dreams, though, and I aim to make 'em come true."

"Okay," I replied, and turned my attention back to the presentation. As the screens and lights came back up, I realized my companion was gone. I figured he'd moved on to his next reenactment.

Mom asked that everyone visit the meditation chapel next door to wait out the rain for a while, so we made their short way there. Along the sidewalk, we passed an outhouse that had been shared not only by the churchgoers but by the families along what was formerly known as Old Saltillo Road. I couldn't imagine walking half a block to use the restroom. It must have been awful, especially if you had to go in the middle of the night.

"I thought it was neat that they had so many people in costume at the church," I ventured as I closed the chapel door behind us.

"That presentation was impressive, all right," Mom settled into one of the pews; unlike the dark wood of the old church, these were golden and bright. "Having screens on the sides to help you feel like it was really happening was a clever way to bring the experience home."

"I wasn't talking about the screens, Mom. I was talking about the people. The couple I saw earlier putting things in that green car outside were there, and the fellow playing their son."

Mom and Dad both looked at me like I'd grown another head.

"Amos," Mom said, "why don't you play something on the piano?"

"I don't know, Diana. It doesn't seem right."

"Well, I don't see any signs saying we can't, and I'd like to hear one of Elvis' hymns if you don't mind."

Dad compromised and sang two verses and a chorus from "Peace in the Valley" a cappella. He used to be a professional singer back in the day, and Mom says she fell in love with him while he was singing an old Cajun song.

I closed my eyes and focused on Dad's voice. In my ear, though, I heard a second voice: the whisper of the boy who'd sat next to me in church.

"Tell your daddy thank you."

I'd always thought that the whole "hair raising on the back of your neck" thing was an old wives' tale, or something that only happened in scary books. But it happened to me right then.

When I opened my eyes, there was no one sitting next to me. However, the sun had come out and was peeping through the stained-glass windows to make colorful swirls on the carpet.

"Let's go over to the house," Mom gamely picked up her cane.

"You guys go ahead," I said. "I want to spend a few more minutes here. I promise I won't be too long."

"All right," Dad said, and helped Mom up and out the door.

After they left, I closed my eyes and spoke aloud.

"I don't know exactly what's going on here, but I'm hoping you'll help me understand."

I opened my eyes, and that same boy was sitting next to me in the pew.

"I reckon your folks can't see me. They seem real nice, though. And I like that your daddy sang for a bit."

"Who are you?"

"You don't know yet? Well, you walk out that door down the pathway to the house and you'll see. Go on now."

I was puzzled, but I went out and followed the pathway.

About halfway between the chapel and the little white house was a circle of park benches and trees. In the middle of the circle was a statue of an overall-clad boy clutching a guitar around the neck. At the base was a plaque reading "Elvis at 13."

My jaw dropped open.

"It's an okay likeness, ain't it?"

The blonde boy materialized next to me, and I got the picture at last.

"But you were grown up when ..."

"When I passed? I surely was. But I left here when I was thirteen. That's why I look this way near the house. Man, I remember what a treat it used to be to sit on the porch and play some new song Brother Smith taught me, or maybe share a Coke and a funny book with one of the fellas. Not that I had so many friends, mind. I was kind of a timid kid. I surely loved Captain Marvel, Junior; he had black hair and wore a jumpsuit with a cape; I thought that was how a hero should look, boy."

Elvis went on to tell me about how no one had much, because all their fathers were sharecroppers. So, if somebody got a funny book, they all passed it around "real careful-like", and how they would even share a bottle of soda pop.

"Oh, hey," he continued, "when you go into that house where I was born, it won't look like much. Hell, it ain't but two rooms, with no 'lectric or running water. They've got it lookin' like it did when we lived there for the most part. At least it's got real wallpaper now, 'stead of newspapers put up with flour and water paste. My mama and daddy worked real hard, and I loved them. We sure didn't have much to speak of, though, like I said. That's why I was so proud to buy my folks a house in Memphis when I got some money.

"Reckon it's time for you to catch up with your folks now, Miss Evie. Thank you for talking with me; sometimes I get lonely for a pretty girl's smile."

"How'd you know my name?"

"Heard your daddy say it, of course. And you knew my name before you got here." He gave me that same lopsided grin. "One more thing. I know what it is to lose my mama, and I know you're worried. Your mama's going to be okay, hear? It's just gonna take some time."

"Thank you, Elvis," I whispered, the tears I'd tried to contain rolling down my cheek. He leaned forward and kissed me where the tears fell; it felt like a gentle breeze against my skin.

I turned toward the tiny shotgun house and walked away from the little park where, if someone were to look closely, they might have thought there were two statues in the circle before deciding it was a trick of the light.

It Happened in Memphis

"Wow! You look like Wanda Jackson or somebody. Gorgeous!" Harvard Chastain actually wolf-whistled when Evie came out of the hotel room.

She'd really gotten into the spirit for their visit to Sun Records; Tante Julie made a fit-and-flare dress, complete with stiff crinolines, in a turquoise print for the occasion. Evie wore it with matching flats and a short white cardigan. Her dark hair was tied up with a white ribbon in a high ponytail that reached to the middle of her back; she'd even found a white and turquoise purse in one of Diana's favorite vintage shops to finish off the outfit. Her cousin Jimmy's girlfriend, Cindy, helped her with black eyeliner winged out in doe eyes and red lipstick that made her look like she'd stepped right out of a 1950s fashion magazine.

"Keep your hair on, couillon," Jimmy teased. "I know for a fact that her daddy knows how to use a shotgun."

Evie's cheeks were beet red with embarrassment.

"Lay off, you guys," Diana said.

To their credit, everyone had behaved themselves after that. Harv had to remind himself that his classmate was just fifteen. He'd been surprised when Evie's parents invited him along to Memphis; like Evie, he loved old music.

Amos maneuvered the van down a narrow alley into the parking lot behind Sun Studio. The energy in the car was palpable; everyone was looking forward to the tour.

"I think you look pretty as a basket of flowers, baby girl," Amos said as they got out of the car and Evie smoothed her skirt.

"Thank you, Daddy. Can you take my picture in front of Jerry Lee?" A big image of the piano player hung next to the studio's back door.

"Of course I can, sweetheart."

Once inside the sweet shop and souvenir store, Amos bought tickets for the first tour of the day. Several people asked if they could take Evie's picture and she posed in the restaurant booth by the window.

"Once this tour gets going," Amos said, "I want cameras and phones put away. I'll take enough pictures for everyone, I promise ... but I want all of you to really enjoy this and see it through something other than your camera lens."

When their tour group was called, Evie and the rest of the family filed into the record shop to listen to the beginning speech. There was a little something about the history of the building, including that where they were standing had been part of Taylor's restaurant. Then, they went upstairs to the museum containing artifacts from the entire history of Sun Studio. BB King's guitar, Ike Turner's wrecked amplifier ... all of it. The guide explained that, at one point, the upstairs portion of the building had pretty much served as a boarding house. The musicians whose names would eventually become household words were so poor that they couldn't afford places to stay on their own and so they slept above the studio in hopes of getting some session work to supplement their contracts. Dell Taylor, who owned the restaurant, would let them eat their "meat and three" on credit, paying up at the end of the week.

Once they all filed downstairs to the studio, Evie felt like they had entered a shrine of some sort. There were photos of Sun artists all over the walls, a line of guitars along one wall, and a stack of antique amplifiers on the floor below the booth window. Two stand-up basses leaned against cabinets. There were three Xs marked in tape on the tan linoleum floor. Over the piano was a huge picture of Elvis Presley, Jerry Lee Lewis, Carl Perkins, and Johnny Cash.

"That's where Elvis stood," the docent explained. "Those other two were where Scotty and Bill sat the night they recorded 'That's Alright Mama.' And I swear to you, Bob Dylan came in here one day and kissed that X where Elvis stood."

The tour culminated with everyone having a chance to handle Elvis Presley's old RCA Shure 77 microphone before filing out to what had been Marion Keisker's office in the 1950s. Harv really hammed it up with the mic. It was then that Evie realized she didn't have her purse.

"I'll be right back, Daddy," she said to Amos. "I'll just grab it and meet you all in the souvenir shop."

She went back up the stairs to the museum first, uncertain of where she'd sat down her little handbag.

"Hey! Y'all want to knock or somethin'?"

The dark-haired man sat up on the little iron-framed bed. "Thank goodness it's been so cold, or I mightn't have had anything on, girl. What you doin' up here?"

"I ... wait. Where's the museum?"

"Museum? Girl, I don't know what you're talkin' about. And you still ain't answered me."

"I thought I left my purse up here."

"Well, you must have been with some other fella, because you didn't leave it under ol' Roy Orbison's bed."

Evie stared at him in shock. "Left it under the bed? Why, I ..." Her cheeks were hot with embarrassment.

It's happening again, just like in Tupelo. Please, let me be wrong. I'm not ready for this.

"Maybe I left it down in the studio. I won't disturb you any further."

Evie went down the stairs that she'd taken just moments before. The studio looked totally different. There were no photos on the walls, no X marks on the floor ... just a group of people milling around. Evie shook her head in confusion.

Over at the piano, a man with dark blond hair sat on the bench with three others gathered around. A long-legged, dark-haired woman in a woolen suit with a pencil skirt sat on the back of the spinet while a man took their photograph.

After the photographer left, one of the men left as well, everyone calling out "So long, Johnny" or something similar as he walked out the door. The man who'd been at the piano helped the young woman down from the back of it and went over to chat with a bunch of friends who'd evidently come with him.

"Whoo-ee, ain't you a pretty thing?" One of the other men who'd been in that big photograph came over to Evie. He had wavy, peroxide-blonde hair and the most arresting amber eyes that Evie had ever seen. "What's your name, baby doll"

"I'm Evangeline Boudreaux. I think I left my purse in here earlier. It's turquoise and white, to go with my dress. I don't imagine you've seen it?"

"I ain't seen no pocketbook, no. But I tell you what; with a name like Evangeline Boudreaux, and that sweet accent of yours, you must be from Louisiana. Guess what? I am, too. Jerry Lee Lewis, from Ferriday. What do they call you at home, baby doll?"

"Evie."

"Nah, that ain't right. That's a little girl's name. Reckon I'll call you Lina. How 'bout that?"

"Sure."

This can't be happening. This has got to be a reenactment of some kind. But they couldn't have taken those photographs down so fast.

"Elvis, Carl, I want you all to meet Lina Boudreaux. She's from Louisiana, too."

Everyone turned around and made polite noises of greeting. Elvis looked a little askance. "When did your date show up, Jerry?"

"Just now. See? You ain't the only one got a pretty girl at your side."

"You got a real pretty wife named Jane, is what I hear." Carl took a long drink from a flask.

"I will have you to know, Mister Perkins, that me and Janie is what you'd call estranged. We are seekin' to divorce."

"Not the first time for you, either, is it?"

"Carl, I don't know what kind of bug you have up you're a— your backside. 'Scuse my language, Miss Lina. But yes, it's my second divorce. Not that it's any of your concern."

This was like no reenactment that Evie could have imagined. Something very strange was going on.

"So, we gonna make this-here 'Matchbox' record of yours or not?" Jerry Lee continued.

His question went unnoticed, as Elvis was talking about seeing a group in Las Vegas, where he'd met Marilyn, called Billy Ward's Dominoes. As he described the singer who had covered "Don't Be Cruel" in such an unexpected way, he started playing and singing. Carl rolled his eyes a little.

"You sit down next to me, Lina." Jerry Lee scooted over on the bench. "Looks like we're gonna be here for a while."

He listened carefully to the key in which Elvis was playing and singing, and then joined in with some fills and runs on the piano.

Oh, my God. It's December 4, 1956. I have just stumbled into the most amazing day in the history of rock music. And there is no way in hell I can tell Harv about this. He'll think I'm insane.

Before long, all three men were playing together, trying to figure out which key a given song was in or remembering pieces that they liked. Jerry Lee and Elvis knew a great many of the same hymns.

"We're both Assemblies of God," Jerry Lee explained to Evie. "Carl, there, he's a Baptist. He don't know all the same songs we come up with."

Nevertheless, Carl Perkins figured out how to play along, putting in just the right rhythm and notes.

Marion poked her blonde head in from her office and asked if the "three rover boys" would play "Farther Along" for her, and they were happy to oblige.

Everyone seemed to be having a good time except Marilyn; Evie thought she looked bored out of her mind. That seemed sad to her, because this was such a historic event.

Still, none of them really knew that yet, did they?

After a while, Elvis and Jerry Lee sang "Peace in the Valley" together, just like Amos and had in the chapel back in Tupelo. Then Elvis started goofing around, trying to remember parts of songs. That gave Jerry Lee his opening.

"Lina, how about if I take you next door to Dell Taylor's place? I'll buy you somethin' to drink and you can hear my record on the juke box. It's only been out three days and I'm real proud of it."

"I'll bet you ain't got but two bits in your pocket, Jerry Lee." Carl took another drink from his flask. "What are you going to do, buy her an RC cola and a Moon Pie?"

Jerry Lee dug into the pocket of his slacks and hauled out some change. "That is every word of a lie, Perkins. I happen to have six bits in my pocket, which is more than enough to get Miss Lina a chocolate milkshake if that's what she wants, and to play my record for her."

"That won't leave you much, will it?"

"No one said I was planning to eat. Now, where's your coat, baby doll?"

"I don't have anything but this sweater."

"That's all right. You can wear mine. We're not going far." Jerry Lee took Evie's hand and led her out through the office. "We'll be right back, Miss Marion," he said to the blonde secretary seated there. He grabbed a cloth jacket from the stand by the door and draped it over Evie's shoulders.

At Taylor's, they sat in the booth right next to the window. Jerry Lee ordered chocolate Cokes for himself and Evie, and then put a nickel in the Wurlitzer jukebox. A rollicking piano introduction rolled out across the room and "Crazy Arms" poured out the speakers. It was followed by the flip side, "End of the Road."

"I reckon I'm gonna be bigger'n Elvis one of these days," he said as the waitress brought the drinks to their table. "Ain't nobody got the talent I do, and I'm only twenty-one. How old are you, Lina?"

"I'm fifteen."

"That's a good age, right there. Just about perfect. You know, you surely are a pretty girl. You've got the bluest eyes I've ever seen. Reckon those came from your mama; your daddy must be Cajun, with a name like Boudreaux. That's where that black hair come from, ain't it?"

"Yes, sir."

"Don't sir me, baby doll. We're on a date, for cryin' out loud. I ain't your daddy."

Evie laughed, and looked down at the table. She could feel herself blushing.

"And I'll bet you ain't never been kissed, have you?"

Evie stared at him. "How did you know?"

"Just a hunch. And I mean to take care of that right this minute." Jerry Lee leaned forward and pressed his mouth to Evie's. "Mm, mm. Sweet as a summer day."

Evie blushed again and took another sip of her drink.

The record ended, and Jerry Lee asked her what she thought.

"It was just amazing, Jerry Lee. Thank you so much. I imagine we should get back to the studio, though."

"You're right." He dropped some coins on the table before wrapping his jacket around Evie's shoulders again. "Say, when Mr. Phillips pays me for this session today, I surely would like to take you someplace for supper. Would you like to join me at the Peabody or somewhere else nice downtown?"

Evie couldn't help herself; she genuinely liked the brash young piano player. "I'd enjoy that very much, Jerry Lee. Thank you."

When they came back in, Elvis was talking to his girlfriend again awhile Carl glowered in the background. Jerry Lee sat down at the piano and started playing "Crazy Arms." Elvis moved the microphone closer to him so that his singing could be heard. Then, Jerry Lee started "That's My Desire," looking deep into Evie's eyes rather than at the piano. Not a note was out of place as he played.

Marilyn asked if he'd play "End of the Road," and Jerry Lee was happy to oblige. Then everyone packed up and saying their goodbyes.

"I don't know what I'm going to do, Jerry Lee," Evie said. "I still haven't found my purse, and I need to get back to where my family's staying."

"Well, if you don't find it, I imagine I could help you get to your folks' hotel. And you don't need your pocketbook for me to take you to dinner. I surely would like to get to know you better, Lina Boudreaux."

Marilyn overheard the conversation and walked over to the piano. "Is your pocketbook sort of blue-green and white?"

"Yes, it is."

"Well, there's one like that right out on Miss Marion's desk."

"Thank you!"

Evie walked out into the office and, sure enough, there was her purse. She picked it up, and walked back into the studio to re-join the musicians. She was looking forward to her dinner date.

There was another tour group listening to the same spiel she'd heard in what now felt like another lifetime. Jerry Lee and the rest of the gang had been gone for decades. Evie walked through the door to the souvenir shop, where her family waited.

"That didn't take long," Jimmy said. "I was afraid you'd get lost in there."

"I think I might have," she replied. Jimmy and Amos exchanged a look, but let it go. She'd talk about it when she felt ready.

"Daddy, may I have something from the record shop?"

"As long as you don't pick something that costs an arm and a leg, I don't see why not. Go ahead."

Evie went into the little room and studied the walls until she found the item she wanted: a 45 RPM record, wrapped in cellophane and attached to a cardboard square.

"That's a good one, honey," Amos said when she handed him the Sun recording of "Crazy Arms" backed with "End of the Road."

The next day, Harv and Evie took the hotel shuttle down to Beale Street to have lunch at Dyer's; Amos had told them that the burgers were made in hundred-year-old grease, and they were curious. They both wore Sun Studio t-shirts and blue jeans. Evie's long, dark hair flowed loose down her back. Harv thought she looked gorgeous, but was afraid to say much of anything after embarrassing himself the day before. After lunch, they walked along the street, Harv regaling Evie with stories from what felt like the entire history of blues.

A tall, elderly man with wavy, steel-grey hair was being helped out of a car just a few feet from where Evie and Harv were standing, and he stared at her with eyes that were still deep brown and piercing. It was clear that every step he took was painful; he leaned on his cane to draw himself up a little taller.

"Lina Boudreaux," he said, just loud enough for Evie to hear. "That can't be right. You must be her granddaughter or something."

Evie excused herself and walked over to the car.

"It's me, Jerry Lee. I don't know how, or why, but it really is me. And I can't thank you enough. You and the rest of the guys did me a great honor." She reached up and dropped a peck on the old man's papery cheek. "I'll never forget who gave me my first kiss."

"And I'll never forget that pretty little girl who stood me up for dinner. Don't tell my wife now, hear?" The great piano player patted her shoulder gently with still-strong hands before he turned away and his wife walked him into the building on Beale Street.

"Do you know who that was," Harv enthused. "Only one of the most important people in Memphis history, and you walked right up to him and gave him a kiss like that? Evie, you never cease to amaze me."

What he didn't tell her was how jealous he was of the way her face lit up when she saw that grey-haired man who was more than old enough to be her grandfather. The feeling confused him too much.

"Harv, I think I'd like it if you called me Lina."

Ghosts of Whitehaven

"Your daddy didn't have to spring for the most expensive tour," Harv whispered to Evie as they waited for the private van. "I'm almost embarrassed at this point, he's paid for so many nice things."

"Harv, he promised your mom she wouldn't have to worry about the expenses on this trip. If it's one thing I know about my dad, he meant that. Just relax and enjoy yourself."

Harv followed Evie onto the little bus. She'd been acting differently since Sun Studios ... not in any way that he could put his finger on, but he sensed it. She was both friendlier and more aloof, like she understood something new about herself. Like she had more experience of the world.

And that didn't make any sense to him.

Harv turned his attention to what their guide was saying as the van entered the famous musical gates of Graceland. This was the moment when one of his dreams was coming true. He'd have been happy just going through the house with an iPad, but Amos had bought the tour with a guide for their group of six ...along with four nice older people from their same hotel. They'd see the grounds, the outbuildings, and even some special items from the archives.

"If we're going to do this thing, let's do it up right," Amos had said when he'd told them about the grand surprise he'd arranged before they ever left New Orleans.

Well, Harv surely couldn't claim Amos was failing to keep his word.

After the short introductory welcome film, the group was given headsets so that they could hear their guide even if they got separated. It was okay to linger a little to take photos and so on, so sometimes visitors had to catch up.

Evie was paying attention to everything the guide said before the front door of Graceland was opened to them. Once they were inside, she couldn't help it; her jaw dropped open at the opulence of Elvis

Presley's adulthood home. It was a far cry from the little house in Tupelo where she'd talked to a ghost in overalls.

The all-white living room, the music room just beyond it ... the dining room with Elvis and Priscilla's wedding china laid out. Evie thought the boy she'd talked to in Tupelo must have been like a kid in a candy store as he furnished the huge home with the finest things money could buy at the time.

The purple and white bedroom at the back, near the kitchen, was still arranged as it was when Vernon and Gladys Presley had lived there, the guide informed her through the headset. The pink poodle wallpaper in the little bathroom had been chosen by Gladys herself, as had the color scheme. Evie thought she saw a black-haired woman in the room, just out of the corner of her eye. The woman was wearing a brocade dress, sensible pumps, and a locket around her neck. When she looked again, there was no one there.

From the photos in the living room, Evie realized that she'd seen a brief glimpse of Gladys Presley; apparently, the Tupelo house wasn't the only one with its ghost.

At the foot of a stairwell, which was roped off so the general public couldn't go up to Elvis' bedroom, bathroom, and office, was a portrait of him with his natural blonde hair; he'd begun dying it so that it would show up better on film and in photos, the guide was explaining. As she took everyone down to the TV room and billiard room, down a little flight of stairs, another voice came into Evie's headset.

"Lina Boudreaux."

Evie did a double-take and tapped on her headset just in case. She double-checked that the channel was still right; it was.

"Lina, wait up. I need to talk to you before the next group comes in. And don't worry, honey; no one else can hear me on that thing."

She looked around her, seeing no one with a microphone.

"Look up the stairs, honey."

Standing there was a man with heavy sideburns and black hair. He was wearing ivory-colored slacks with a thin, matching belt, and a silk shirt printed in an abstract pattern of black, blue and red dots. The shirt was clearly custom-made, with elastic around the biceps and wrists, which ended in a ruffle; Evie remembered reading in the Tupelo museum that the star had his shirts made that way so the cuffs wouldn't slip down when he played piano or guitar. He was a little thicker-waisted than the young star she'd met at Sun Records, but there was no mistaking him.

"Yes, it's really me." Elvis gave her a little half-smile that lit his sleepy blue eyes. "And you're the only one who can see me. I won't keep you long."

He came down the stairs to stand next to her, staying on his side of the velvet rope. "I can't come downstairs during the day. It's like I'm trapped up here until the doors are locked for the night. Not sure why, but after that I can go where I want to. And, sometimes people can see me. Usually they just shake their heads and don't believe it ... but you know better."

"I do indeed. You called me Lina ..."

"That's how Jerry Lee introduced you way back when. I could tell you liked it. And I hear ol' Jerry Lee was mad as hell that his pretty girl up and disappeared instead of going out to dinner with him all those years ago."

"I'm a little bit in shock right now."

"I imagine so. Come over here a little bit closer, will you?"

Evie got as close to the rope as she could, and Elvis put his arms around her in a hug that she would remember for the rest of her life.

"Everything's going to be just fine, Lina. You wait and see. Your mama and them are going to be okay, even when health things feel hard. And that young fellow Harv? Whether you want to believe it or not, he's the one for you."

"Harv would never understand what I'm going through, seeing you here and in Tupelo, and going for a soda with Jerry Lee Lewis before I was ever even born. I can't tell him about that, ever … let alone that Jerry Lee gave me my first kiss."

"You'll know when the time is right, honey. And let me tell you something; you just never know what people will or won't understand. When I bought this house for my mama, the neighbors hated us. Called us white trash. Hell, the biggest hero in Whitehaven was a little girl who twirled a baton and became a beauty queen; they even had her name up on the welcome sign. I didn't set out to be no hero, I just wanted to make my mama happy. People didn't understand me in those days, but they sure try to do it now. Speaking of which, they're fixin' to open that door again and you need to catch up with your group. Just remember, this is all real and you're not crazy. You're a special young woman, and I'm glad to have met you."

He didn't walk back up the stairs so much as he faded away into the wall when the front door opened again.

Evie took a long, loving look at the portrait of Elvis as a young man and smiled. She could only ponder what he'd said as she caught up with her group in the billiard room.

Harv didn't ask where she'd been; something about the look on her face, half smiling and not quite there with the rest of them, made him decide to wait.

Hard-Boiled Blues

The Axe Man Cometh

I don't know why y'all adults are always trying to scare the hell out of little kids.

With my Irish Granny O'Halloran, it was always the bainsidh, who would come and get you in the outhouse if you were naughty. With my Cajun Granny Broussard, it was always the rougarou who would get you and take you out to the swamp if you misbehaved or back-sassed your elders.

I think I was ten years old when I stopped to think about how stupid this was.

Wait. We don't even have an outhouse; we've got indoor plumbing. And if some alligator-headed man shows up to take me to the swamp, well, I reckon I'd better go ... and use my daddy's camera to take pictures if I can. That Ripley fellow might talk about it on the radio if I can prove it's true, and I might make a little money for the family. I'm sure those "Believe It Or Not" fellows would love a picture of the rougarou.

Plus, I grew up in the Quarter. We have neighbors who swear they remember Marie Laveau and the yellow snake she called Le Grand Zombi, even though she died fifty years ago. Every other house around here is haunted, including ours if my grannies are to be believed, and I've never seen or heard a thing.

Now, I see you want to interrupt me, but I need to get this story out. You go on and make notes on that little pad of yours, but you've got to wait until I get to the end.

As I started to say before, my cousin Cubby Thibodeaux gets real worried about that bainsidh and rougarou stuff. He asks someone to stand outside the bathroom when he goes in, and he stays away from Bayou St. John and Bayou Metairie when we go to City Park for family picnics. God help us if Cubby has to use the outhouse up there; he practically wants an armed guard. Plus, you can forget about him getting on the Cemeteries street car just to go up there on our own. No sir, not gonna happen.

Cubby's what some folks call simple. That means he'll believe just about any damn thing you tell him. It also means he's repeated the sixth grade four times. He finally got promoted to the seventh grade, and he's 16 years old.

So, I really don't know what got into my Uncle Clarence on one of those picnics I mentioned just now, because he decided to talk about the New Orleans Axe Man. Unlike the bainsidh or the rougarou, the Axe Man was real.

According to Uncle Clarence, the Axe Man got himself good and mad about the Italian folks running grocery stores in the Quarter. Heck, my folks still refer to the part of the Quarter from Jackson Square down to Decatur as Little Palermo, so you know there was a bunch of them. Matter of fact, Italians owned half the grocery stores in the whole city.

Anyway, the Axe Man would go into people's houses at night and split their skulls with a hatchet. No joke. Four of those folks died, including a little girl, and some folks went to the hospital. The first killings happened in an Italian bakery over on Laharpe and Dorgenois; the people lived in the back, and that's where they found the bodies.

For a while, the police chief blamed an elderly neighbor of those first victims ... but that turned out not to be so. Some folks thought it was the Black Hand, but a policeman who knew a lot about the Mafia said the Black Hand wouldn't have left any survivors. Never did find out who did those killings, although I think it was probably another grocer who got mad about the competition, you know?

Yes sir, I can tell by the look on your face that you know just what I'm talking about. I bet your mama taught you that interrupting isn't nice, though, so you let me finish, hear?

Well, Uncle Clarence can't leave well enough alone with just talking about these crimes. No, he's got to go Granny O'Halloran and Granny Broussard one better ... and he tells us that the Axe Man is just waiting around the corner to get children who don't act right.

I just laugh it off; there haven't been any axe murders in more than ten years, and I don't think that fellow is just hanging around the neighborhood with a hatchet, waiting to strike. That doesn't make any sense; he'd be caught by passers-by six days a week and twice on Sunday if that were the case.

But Cubby, he takes it real serious. He starts acting funny whenever the Thibodeaux cousins come to visit. He's extra careful to mind his manners, ask for a guard outside the bathroom, and stay away from the water. But now he wants to walk ahead of me and peep around corners to make sure the coast is clear. You never can tell, is what Cubby says when I ask why the hell he's acting like the Axe Man is waiting over by Café du Monde when we go over there with the dime Granny O'Halloran gave us so we can get some beignets and a glass of milk. Then he says that he thinks my dress is real pretty, and that he can hardly tell Granny Broussard made it out of a flour sack because of the flower print. Granny O'Halloran found a spool of blue thread in her sewing basket that matched those flowers perfectly; she used it to do the tatting around the sleeves. He says I look pretty in it, because the flowers and lace match my eyes. The dress looked almost as good as one from the Maison Blanche department store.

I know it's not so pretty right now, but it was. I promise.

I'm getting to the point, but I think you need to know all of this.

See, Cubby started carrying a pearl-handled jackknife with him. He carries a mess of other stuff with him, like fish hooks and twine and what-not. He keeps that knife sharp with a whetstone from his daddy's tool shed. He says you never can tell when you need a fish hook, some twine, or a jackknife, because the Axe Man just might be out there around the corner. So, you need to protect yourself in case he mistook you for a misbehaving kid, or maybe for an Italian grocer like the fellow who makes the muffalettas. Cubby loves those sandwiches; he likes the olive salad, and would probably eat it out of the jar with a spoon if he had a chance.

Cubby particularly worries about the muffaletta man, but the Central Grocery clerks told him to clear off out of their doorway. He was hanging around there a lot. Plus, you might guess that he's a pretty big kid for being in the seventh grade, and that can look intimidating even when Cubby means well.

Anyway, after we had our beignets and milk, Cubby walked me back to the house. We live up on Dumaine, just off of Burgundy. It's the other side of the Quarter from Café du Monde, but it's not that long a walk. Cubby made sure I got home safe, repeating over and over that you just never know about the Axe Man.

Now, we didn't go directly home. I'm not going to lie. See, there was a whole bunch of guys playing jazz down at Jackson Square, and Cubby wanted to see if Buddy Bolden, Sidney Bechet, or Kid Ory were there. He loves their records. I didn't have the heart to tell him that King Bolden died in the nuthouse, and Bechet and Ory left town years ago. So, we listened to some fellows play. Even if they weren't as cool as those other cats, they were still good.

Anyway, Cubby sees me home and then he says he's gonna go hear those guys play some more. He puts on his porkpie hat, grabs his spoons and says he figures they might let him sit in. Whatever else you can say about Cubby, he can play those spoons pretty good. He always has a good time doing it, too.

After a while, Granny Broussard tells me I need to go fetch Cubby home. It's getting on for supper time, and she wants him back in the house. So, I go outside and I walk toward Jackson Square. I could go straight down St. Ann if I wanted to, but I want to stick to the shade. So, I go down the alley between the cathedral and the Presbytère. That's where I see the body. I shake my head like it's a nightmare, and that body doesn't go away. I see something else, too ... and I decide that maybe I'll go on back to our house on Dumaine and sit on the porch glider to figure out what it means if I'm right. I don't mind telling you, I was praying to Jesus that what I thought I saw was wrong.

Murder in the Quarter isn't news, I guess. It's just business as usual. But what I thought I saw? That made it a whole different matter, and one that I had to consider careful-like. And I still hoped I was wrong.

Granny Broussard comes out and asks me where Cubby is, and I tell her a half-truth. I tell her that I didn't see him but will look out for him again later. Granny Broussard goes back into the house muttering about no-account simple boys and lazy girls.

I don't much care, though. I'm trying to figure out what Nancy Drew would do if she saw what I'd seen. I read those stories from the school library, see, and she's real smart about figuring out what's what. I don't come up with too many ideas, though.

So, maybe an hour goes by and Cubby comes running home. He's lost his porkpie hat, which he's pretty proud of because he figures it makes him look like a real jazz man. I have no idea what became of his spoons.

"Charlene," he hollers as he comes up the street. "I need you to come. It's urgent."

So, I get up from the porch glider and Cubby grabs my hand. "We got to do something."

Cubby drags me down to the alley between the cathedral and the Presbytère, and there's that body I saw before. The guy is laying there in a puddle of blood with Cubby's pearl-handled jackknife stuck straight into his throat and his saxophone flung off to the side. The smell of that blood coming off the hot cobblestones is like when Cubby's pa slaughters a hog. I'm surprised I didn't get sick.

"I thought he was the Axe Man when he came around the corner, Charlene. I swear to Jesus. I saw him carrying that horn and I thought it was his axe. I saw the sun glint off the metal, and I was certain sure. So, I didn't even think straight. I just struck out. I kept yelling that I'd been good. And then he just fell down, throwing his horn over there. What'm I gonna do, Charlene?" Cubby's bouncing back and forth from one foot to the other, like a little kid who needs to use the toilet. "What if it's Kid Ory?"

"Kid Ory plays the trombone, Cubby. Don't be a damn fool."

I roll my eyes at Cubby. Then, I get down on my knees just in case there's a chance that this guy might be alive. I remember something from Girl Scouts about how to feel the pulse in your neck, so I put my fingers in the same place on that man's neck. It doesn't feel anything like my own neck; he feels rubbery.

Now, I see you're wondering about why I didn't do that in the first place. I ain't Nancy Drew, okay? I got scared, and I got gone.

There's no pulse to feel, but I got that guy's blood all over the new dress Granny Broussard made. That's why it isn't so pretty now. Granny Broussard is going to wear me out over this. She may even call in the rougarou. I won't blame her if she does.

Anyway, I told Cubby he had to wait there while I walked all the way up Royal Street to Station House Number Eight. Far as I know, he's still sitting there. Cubby does what I tell him to.

And that's why I'm at your desk, sir. I need you to come arrest Cubby Thibodeaux for what he did to that man. And then I need you to help me explain all of this to the grannies, including why what happened to my new dress isn't my fault. We need to especially ask Granny Broussard not to fetch the rougarou, even if it meant I could take pictures. Then, we need to tell my mama and daddy that I did my best to look after Cubby, but I'm only fourteen and can't do everything. After that, we can try to explain it to Cubby's folks, who are staying up at our place on Dumaine. And to Cubby, which is not going to be easy. After all, he's simple.

Sundown Town

I didn't rightly plan to land up in Memphis. I just knew that when I got out of the Army I couldn't stay in Ferriday, Louisiana. I've seen too much to be kept down like I would be there, you know?

I was part of the 761st Tank Battalion, called into action by Old Blood and Guts Patton himself. We were all colored fellas, which is why they called us the Black Panthers, but ol' Patton didn't care about that. All he cared about was could we shoot or not. So, off to Europe we went. Turns out, white folks in Europe think we're no different from anybody else. Only American white folks talk about us like we're monkeys swingin' from the trees instead of civilized folks. We've got our own colleges and everything else; one fellow in our group got himself a history degree at Dillard University in New Orleans; it was nice to have someone from my home state in the gang. He was one of the smartest fellas I ever got to know; made me wish my folks could have afforded for me to get past high school. That man got hurt real bad and went stateside before I got out.

Anyway, once the war was over and I packed up my uniform and medals to come home, I knew I didn't want to live in the segregated South any more. I didn't want to hear a white man call me "boy" when I'm a grown man and a veteran, you know?

So, first I thought I'd take myself up to Illinois. I heard there were a lot of good jobs up there in factories, especially around a place called Naperville. So, I got myself a bus ticket, hugged my mama goodbye at the Ferriday Greyhound station, and went on my way.

Like I said, I don't have any education beyond high school, and lucky to have that much, but I can do anything I'm given a chance to. So, after all them days on the bus, I found a rooming house that allows me a bath and a chance to shine my shoes and press my shirt before I go calling on any factories. It's in a little area just across the railroad tracks from the "Welcome to Naperville" sign that gives the population and what-not.

First thing my landlady said is this: "You make sure you're out of Naperville by six o'clock at night when they blow that whistle. Assuming they give you a job at all. Otherwise, there's no telling what will become of you."

Well, it turns out to be better than average advice. The only job they're willing to offer me at the factory, with all my experience fixing motors and whatnot, is sweeping up for two dollars a day. They tell me that I should "feel grateful to get it, boy," and before long I'm packing up my little cardboard suitcase and trying again. They claim they couldn't afford to keep me on, but I saw 'em hire a whole mess of white men for more money than I got paid.

Again and again. Anna. Jonesboro. Detroit. Same story every damn where.

I didn't rightly expect to find things up north the way I did. Fact is, things were a little better down south than up north ... and that came as a surprise to me.

I kept up writing letters to some of my friends from the Army, and one fellow, Rudy, allowed as how he got himself a good job waiting tables at a place called the Starlight Lounge in Memphis. Place is up on the top floor of the Hotel Peabody, and he says the tips are good. He says I can stay with his family while I get on my feet, long as I don't mind that he has a couple of sisters who might pester me. Plus, he says that this fellow Crump, who pretty much runs the town, is looking to put a police station on Beale Street so there'll be some colored cops. He said that they were giving preference to veterans, so maybe that would suit me.

So, I packed up my bag again, got a cold chicken lunch tied up in a shoebox from my landlady, and the latest Green Book to show me where it was okay to spend the night if I need to.

Next news you know, I'm getting off the Trailways bus in Memphis, with my buddy Rudy meeting me at the station. He's got the prettiest woman I've ever seen with him, light-skinned, wearing a bright green dress with white spots and a matching sweater thrown over her shoulders. Her hair's fixed nice and she's wearing lipstick.

"This is my sister, Ida," he says as he grabs my suitcase. "She insisted on coming along. Ida, this hot mess here is my Army buddy, Marcus, I've been telling you about."

"Pleasure to meet you, Miss Ida." I tip my hat.

"Likewise," she replies.

"Maybe after I get my things settled, we can get an ice cream or something. Get to know each other better."

"I can't think of anything I'd like more, Marcus," she replies as I open the car door for her. "A. Schwab's, down to Beale Street, is a nice place."

I believe moving to Memphis will turn out to be a real good deal.

The Jade Palace and What Happened There

It's dangerous down in Bronzetown. That's no lie. If you don't know where you're going, you're likely to get rolled, maybe shivved ... or worse. You don't go where you got no business going, and you keep steppin' once your business is done.

I'm gonna tell you about what happened in this chop suey joint over on Gayoso. Chinese fellow opened it up over there, calling it the Jade Palace. Wanted to talk it up to sound finer than it was, to my way of thinking. Anyhow, the place used to be a dinette called Sally's. You could get a decent burger there for a dime, or a meat and three for fifty cents. But Sally got sick and couldn't run the place anymore, so she closed it up and went to live with her sister across the river in West Memphis. That's in Arkansas, in case you're unfamiliar with our geography 'round here.

Anyway, this Charlie Wong fellow come out here from San Francisco, with the idea of gettin' rich with this restaurant. Thing is, Memphis don't have a Chinatown. We got Bronzetown, and the rest of town. But that don't stop Mister Charlie. He buys that spot over on Gayoso, and gets himself a neon sign that says "Jade Palace," with a picture of a Chinaman in a pointy hat pullin' a cart. It commences to flashin' up there on Gayoso. He put a menu up in the window, letting people know they can get their egg foo yung, chop suey, and some damn thing called moo goo gai pan seven days a week. He's got a section for white and colored, so he's good with the law.

Rumor has it that he's also got a card room in the back, playing Chinese gambling games like fan-tan and pai-gow. I never really cottoned to cards, truth be told. Rather take an honest swindle like the one-armed bandits down in my hometown of Ferriday. Haney's Big House has 'em all along the walls. But that's a story for another time.

Anyway, ol' Charlie Wong, it seems like he fails to pay attention to certain things. See, Boss Crump—you've probably heard of him, in that song by ol' Handy if not in the newspaper—he's got what amounts to a machine here in town. He gets things done, and if you want to get things done, well, you need to put some money into the machine. Ol' Charlie Wong doesn't see the need to do that. Crump's machine operates mostly in Bronzetown, on Beale Street in particular. Like I said, Wong's establishment is over on Gayoso. He thinks that being one block away from the machine means he's immune from it, I guess.

There's a handful of chop suey joints over on Beale, and a couple on Hernando. Charlie Wong figures he got the prime spot, because it's closer to the Peabody and places like that; he reckons he'll get more white folks coming in there. Plus, him being Chinese—even though he was born in San Francisco – I guess he figures he's more authentic than the colored cats runnin' the Pagoda or the Rickashaw House. So, he goes putting on airs when he walks down to Beale Street to buy some chickens or whatever he needs for the restaurant that day. He wears a fine suit, almost nice as the ones at Lansky Brothers, and he struts along the sidewalk like he's the best thing that ever was. He smiles at all the folks, white or colored, and wishes them good morning like they're all friends. Truth is, most folks ain't too fond of ol' Charlie Wong. He's gettin' above his raisin', is what the colored folks say. White folks just think he's a different-shade of colored man, so far as I can tell, so they roll their eyes and keep on steppin' unless they're in the Jade Palace for a plate of the greasy noodles he calls chow mein and a hand of cards in the back.

I tell you all that to say it's hard to know who he pissed off the most. Hell, for all I know, it could have been some woman. There's not a man alive who doesn't know how bad an idea it is to piss off a woman; they'll get you ten ways from Sunday if they've got a mind to. My Ida, she's a good woman. Attends the Clayborn A.M.E. Church every week, and is bringin' up our daughter to be a lady. Her sister, Rose, though, is a whole other story; she's a bear cat. I saw her fetch a knot in her man Cletus' head one time when she got good and mad at him. Took more'n a week for that lump to settle down. Now, Clete ain't much to write home about to begin with; Ida says he look like he got hit with a board as a child and never got well. But he loves Rose, so he stays.

But that's a story for another time, too.

What I do know is what happened.

One Friday night, the door of the Jade Palace is still locked. There're people waiting outside, believe it or not, some of 'em even banging on the door. Some of the folks're all dressed up; there's shows at the Orpheum and the Hippodrome that night that they've already paid their dollar to see, and the fellas want to impress their ladies with some of this fancy foreign food that ol' Charlie Wong serves up.

Well, someone finally decides to call for a policeman. Closest station is over on Beale Street, so they come and got me. Guess a black copper is better than nothin' sometimes. So, there I go up to Gayoso. I tell all the people to calm down and I'll look into the matter.

First thing I do, I go into the back alley behind the Jade Palace. Every restaurant and bar has a back entrance for the help, deliveries, and what-not. And what do I see but that back door wide open. Now, I got me a night stick, but I also got me a gun that I'm not rightly supposed to have, and a straight razor. I know I can defend myself if I need to.

All the same, I ask the white fella who came and got me to go in with me, so I got a witness that I didn't do or touch anything I shouldn't. So, he follows me in. Radio's playin' that Bee Bee King's show, with him talkin' about Jimmy Lunceford's records. Strikes me as odd that Charlie Wong listens to Bee Bee King on radio station WDIA, but there you go. You never know with some folks.

And there's Charlie himself, lying face-up on the floor with a big carving knife stickin' out from between his ribs. I know right away no woman did this; it takes strength to put a knife like that into a fellow. Those things aren't made for stabbing; they're made for slicing. So, you'd have to drive it in hard and fast. He ain't been moved since he was stabbed, either; blood's all pooled around him instead of spread out. He died where he fell.

I also notice the cash box standin' on the counter, empty as a school house in July. Ol' Charlie Wong won't need that money any more, but I make a note of it all the same. I also notice there's no cooks or waiters to be seen, which is mighty peculiar in a restaurant.

There's no use pretending Charlie's going to the hospital to get better. Lucky for him, though, he's got a telephone right there on the kitchen wall. So, I get on the phone and call the white police station over on Main, give 'em my badge number, and tell 'em what I found in the Jade Palace over on Gayoso. The dispatcher heaved a sigh and promised to send another copper and the meat wagon. I told him how I came to be there, and he told me to keep the white fellow who fetched me there, and send the other folks on about their way. Won't be any chop suey happenin' tonight in this place.

So, the white fellow, he gets pretty pissed off. Says he's got tickets for the show at the Orpheum for him and his lady friend. I talk to the both of them, tell her to go on to the show and her gentleman will be along directly.

The two of us wait with ol' Charlie Wong's mortal remains until the other policeman and the coroner's car get here. There's no Chinese hospital here in Memphis, so the driver isn't sure where to take the body. Negro hospital won't take him, and neither will Baptist. We all know this.

We also know that Charlie Wong's murder and the robbery won't be investigated worth a damn. What's left of him will lay up in the city morgue until the white police say there's nothing more they can do about the matter and he winds up in a pauper's grave at the back of Elmwood Cemetery.

I think about trying to find out who his people were in San Francisco, so someone can let them know. Ida, though, she points out that we don't even know where to start. 'Sides, she says, chances are better than even that he ran afoul of ol' Boss Crump, and we can't afford that.

When it's all said and done, my life doesn't change any. I'm back on Beale Street, policing my people the best I can and keepin' my head down. And ol' Charlie Wong isn't pissing anyone off anymore.

Sometimes, that's just how it happens in Memphis.

Check Out the Other Titles
That Inspired Some of These Stories

In The Eye of The Beholder
In The Eye of The Storm
Bayou Fire

Last Stop: Storyville, originally published by Smashwords, Inc., 2018. ISBN

97-80463803400.

Yellowjack and the River Man, originally published by Smashwords, Inc., 2018. ISBN

97-80463573105.

A Light Across the Lake, originally published by Smashwords, Inc., 2018. ISBN

97-80463880821. Previously published as "Nous Sommes Deux Heures" and "Nous Sommes Quatorze Heures" in *Twelve Hours Later*, Treehouse Writers (2015), and Thinking Ink Press (2017).

Down on the Corner of Love, originally published by Smashwords, Inc., 2019. ISBN

9780463533994.

Two Days in June, originally published by Smashwords, Inc., 2019. ISBN

9780463198841. Previously published in *Thirty Days Later*, Thinking Ink Press, 2016.

Flowers of Europe, originally published by Smashwords, Inc., 2019. ISBN

9780463581629. Previously published published as "Flowers of London" and "Flowers of Paris" in *Some Time Later*, Thinking Ink Press, 2017.

It Happened in Memphis, originally published by Smashwords, Inc., 2019. ISBN

9780463022788. "Ghosts of Tupelo" previously published in *Dark Visions*, Great Oak Publishing, 2018.

Hard-Boiled Blues, originally published by Smashwords, Inc., 2020. ISBN

9780463924495.

About the Author

Award-winning author Sharon E. Cathcart (she/her) writes historical fiction with a twist! A former journalist and newspaper editor, Sharon has been writing for as long as she can remember and always has at least one work in progress. She is a member of the Archaeological Institute of America, Historical Novel Society, and Sisters in Crime. Sharon lives in the Silicon Valley, California, with her very patient husband and several rescue cats.

Read more at sharonecathcart.wordpress.com.